DANIEL'S
PRIDE

Jerome S. Walford

Cover art by Jerome S. Walford
ISBN: 0988611465
ISBN 13: 9780988611467 (Paperback)
9780988611474 (ebook)

Forward Comix
Brooklyn, New York
www.forwardcomix.com

Special thanks to my editors,
Jack Sheedy,
Maya Rock, and
Rebekah Griffin Greene.

Dedicated to
my loving and patient wife, Amy Walford,
and our Rambun-shialon-ctious
Kayla, Charles, and Colette.

CURSE OF THE GRIFFIN
Jerome S. Walford

PART I
DANIEL'S PRIDE

Everyone should have friends.
At least one person who knows you, knows where you should
be and where you shouldn't.
And when that friend has found you astray, will bring you
home at any cost.
—William Griffin, *The Scrolls of Wisdom*

CONTENTS

CHAPTER 1
SHINY OBJECTS

U nder the cover of the early morning haze, Daniel reached the monumental bank building made of carved stone. He felt insignificant beside it. The two massive gargoyle statues seemed to stare down at him as he clutched the strap of his khaki shoulder bag. Daniel entered the vaulted lobby. He adjusted his beanie hat as he walked up to the customer line and wrapped his tattered, moss green jacket more tightly around his chest. There were only three customers ahead, all quite a bit older than him.

The woman in front of Daniel looked over her shoulder, gave a grim smile, and then sheepishly looked down. She was probably in her forties, but it was hard to be certain. Her hair was unkempt. Her skin was taut over her skeletal frame and covered in splotches of a red rash.

She looked at Daniel once more. "Is this your first time?" she asked with a raspy voice. Daniel nodded. "This is my fourth," she continued. "It's a good service—you just shouldn't use it too often, that's all."

Daniel looked ahead at the glossy red kiosks. They had a sleek and sexy design, almost certain to still have that new-equipment scent and pristine shine. There were three machines standing side by side, allowing just a small amount of elbowroom per customer with waist-high dividers between the stations. The glowing sign just above the machines read "We're All Family Here."

Another man finished and stepped away. He rolled down his sleeves and placed a folded stack of blue-backed bills in his interior jacket pocket. The man ahead of the woman stepped in front of the now-empty slot.

In the commonwealth of Anthrazit, the severe work shortage had many in its grip. These new machines at First Central Bank were part of a new initiative, a gesture to provide some resources for those with dwindling options.

The man interacted with the kiosk for a short time. The screen chimed, "For Unturned Customers Only." The man rolled up the sleeve of his right arm, held it over the machine, and took a deep breath.

A thin, snakelike tube wormed its way from the blood currency machine (BCM) and struck at the man's hand. The tube inserted a thin injection needle and sucked with extreme force. The blood slithered up through the transparent tube and into the BCM.

"Ah, that burns," the man exclaimed. He reached up and gripped the divide that separated him and the next customer.

Daniel's eyes widened in panic, and he turned swiftly, bumping into the customer waiting behind him. He ran out of the lobby and walked hurriedly away from the bank, not sure where he was going or what he was going to do next. Daniel eventually came to a bench and sat down; he tugged on his hat to make sure his ears were still covered, and panted rapidly.

"I've seen that look before. You aren't the first to freak out." The observer was a middle-aged man with cropped blond hair. He was dressed in a dark pinstriped suit and stood confidently with his hands in his pant pockets. His pale skin was the first giveaway, and then a slight grin revealed his subtle fangs. He sat next to Daniel, looking into the distance, draping his arm over the back of the bench. Daniel regarded him cautiously.

"There was a time when you could arrive in Anthrazit with a few bills in your pocket and pull yourself up by your bootstraps, if you were hardworking. Not anymore," the man commented. He sighed and turned to look at Daniel, who reacted by looking downward. "I can tell you are not from Central District—you lack that kind of polish, and you don't have the furnace tanning of an Industrial District resident laborer."

Daniel slowly pulled away, clutching his shoulder bag. The stranger stuck out his hand, and Daniel hesitantly returned the handshake. The pale stranger grabbed Daniel's hand and held on firmly, not planning to let go.

"Life as a commoner from South Central affords few choices, if any at all," he remarked. "My name is Cesar Blake. What's yours?"

"My name is Daniel, Daniel Griffin."

Cesar's cold hand did not relax its hold on Daniel, who hadn't budged since he made it to his feet.

"Have a seat, Daniel," Cesar invited, and Daniel obeyed. He was obviously an accomplished vampire, midlevel management at least, and Daniel hoped he would soon lose interest. Daniel's survival instincts told him to play dead and make no sudden moves. He would be as boring as possible.

"A young man such as you should be finishing up grade school, getting ready to apply to a trade school, or looking for a decent job," Cesar stated. "Not in line at a BCM."

"I just needed some quick bills to enter a contest. It's no big deal," Daniel replied almost flippantly.

"You mean the South Central Animal Preserve art contest?" Cesar responded. "Even folks in Central District are talking about it. I'm pretty sure it's the only one around worth a first encounter with one of those things." He grinned slickly. "There's a lot of competition.

Central Arts Tech will have a strong showing. Those students are the real deal. Do you have what it takes?" Cesar prodded.

Daniel displayed no interest in his companion's accomplished exterior and no fire of his own—nothing that would persuade Cesar to risk forcibly turning him. By law, only true blood vampires could turn someone against their will, and Daniel guessed correctly that Cesar was not one.

"A starving artist, huh? I should've known. Those cutout gloves you're wearing should have been my first clue," Cesar replied with a hint of admiration.

This made Daniel wonder just how long Cesar had been stalking him. He hoped that the stranger's break would be over soon.

"Do you believe in fate?" Cesar asked.

"I don't know. I guess." Daniel shrugged.

"What if I told you that I know Jessica Winters?" Cesar said. His final bait was perfect.

"I love her work. She's amazing," Daniel blurted out.

"She is the deciding vote in the competition. As it turns out, she will be attending a special drink ceremony tonight, and I'll be hosting it. Just a little inner-circle welcome for Leonardo, your newly appointed district governor. It is pretty full, though..."

Cesar paused and reached into his inner jacket pocket. He pulled out a glossy brochure and a business card.

"Do you have a pen?"

Daniel began to rummage through his khaki shoulder bag, while Cesar looked around. Across the street was a fifty-foot silver spire that rose out of the sidewalk. It was a communication relay, one of many that could be found throughout Anthrazit. They emitted faint buzzing sounds that were barely noticeable to Commoners, but had a strangely hypnotic effect on young, undisciplined vampires. Cesar spotted a group of vampire teens that had begun to loiter around the relay spire. They stared at it; one got close and began rubbing his forehead against it.

As Daniel dug deep into his bag, Jessica Winters' award-winning book, *"Winters in the Wilderness"*, fell out like an embarrassing confession. Cesar chuckled. The book was powder blue with a picture of a large lioness on the cover. Daniel quickly picked up the book and shoved it into his bag. After fumbling a while longer, he produced a well-used pencil.

Cesar jotted some information on the back of the card. "The only thing I ask is that you keep an open mind tonight," he prefaced, handing both the brochure and the card to Daniel. With a parting tap on the shoulder, Cesar got up and briskly crossed the street toward the vampire teens. "Don't you kids have a training session to attend?"

As Cesar turned his attention elsewhere, Daniel quietly rushed away.

CHAPTER 2

ANIMALS AND OTHER WILD THINGS

Rush hour had begun, and the stampede of pedestrians pressed in on Daniel, who tried to pick up his pace. He heard a series of grunts from behind as Commoners knocked others aside in their big hurry.

"Watch it!" a woman snapped as though she would bite his head off.

Daniel gained speed, but he could not help the occasional stare into the faces of the crowd. Everyone was in such close proximity to each other, yet no one made eye contact or said "good morning" or "hello" to their fellow travelers. This was the norm in Anthrazit. The Commoners' motto was "Work hard, keep your head down, and walk with a quickness in your step."

Daniel looked up. Smog blocked out any view of the other side of the street. The milky-white substance drifted lower just ahead so that he could hardly see more than thirty feet beyond his nose. The air had the lingering odor of a strong cleaning fluid, the kind that was meant for cleaning the dirtiest of objects but always left a distinct smell of its own that needed to be removed.

It was not uncommon to get a rash or develop an itch from exposure to the air, much as the woman from the bank had exhibited. As a result, most people wore high-collared sweaters with zippers to bring the collar to a closed position over their noses and mouths. Others wore turtlenecks, scarves, or shawls when navigating the most-polluted parts of Anthrazit. Goggles weren't usually necessary, but were occasionally worn by teens as a fashion must-have.

The sidewalks were wide to accommodate the mad, dashing pedestrian population. Their footsteps clacked and tapped loudly against the grimy cobblestone. Beyond the sidewalks were narrow streets, along which a few vehicles called "mobiles" tracked along.

The mobiles had four wheels in back and a pair in front. Each wheel was a metal disc wrapped in dense bands of rubber. They had long hoods to house the large, coal-based engine that powered the vehicle's motion and elongated metal exhaust pipes running alongside. Personal mobiles sat one person comfortably. Two was a tight fit, and three was possible if you were completely desperate. Technological development was stifled in this densely populated region, and mechanical objects were luxury items, personal mobiles particularly so. Oversized mobiles (typically referred to as over-mobiles) looked very similar to personal ones, save for large containers fitted at the rear for transporting various goods through the districts.

With no apparatus to manage the flow of traffic, the mobiles made their way along joltingly, stopping as pedestrians spilled into the roadway. "You mechanical beast," a defiant person lashed out.

The rabid daily exchange continued as drivers honked viciously, and the mobiles would froth with burnt coal dust when they got going again. Daniel wrapped his scarf around his nose as he approached the next intersection.

"Stay above ground," advised speakers mounted on a pole at the intersection. The announcement was followed by loud static and indiscernible squawking sounds, supposed news items of the day.

The next group of mobiles was a small distance away, and Daniel hurriedly crossed the street, breaking loose of the pedestrian herd. He felt a moment of freedom from the jockeying of his fellow pedestrians.

On this side of the street was a park, although it was more a quiet pasture than anything else. There were just a few benches at the entrance and several wilted, brownish patches of grass. Daniel began to study how different the mood was compared to the rush-hour side; instead of hurried frenzy, there was a burdensome melancholy.

There was a man sitting on the next bench in full corporate dress: a tailored suit with a matching overcoat and just a hint of a statement with a cheery pink tie. But he sat motionless, bleakly clutching his briefcase with no work to attend to. Further down a sloped path appeared another figure, a young woman. She was stunningly gorgeous, able to attract long gazes, but she wore her beaten-down and broken spirit like a shroud, peering into the distance with a vacant stare.

As the path continued, he found other figures sitting solemnly, each with a unique story. Then Daniel reached the sign that marked his destination. It was an obnoxious green metal billboard, covered in dripping rust stains, that read: *You Are Now Leaving Central District.*

Daniel looked around eagerly for the mass transport. He checked his pockets to confirm that he still possessed the required boarding ticket and sat down on the bench just to the right of the sign.

After a moment, he opened the bag and pulled out Jessica Winters's book. The imposing image of the lioness left very little room for anything else on the cover. The title, *Winters in the Wilderness,* was imprinted in gold foil at the bottom. The book had many dog-eared pages; Daniel opened it to scan the many underlined paragraphs. He read one passage silently, mouthing the words:

> *My relationship with this magnificent creature is one of respect. If we have any hope of restoring our severed connection with nature, we must show its ambassadors the utmost level of respect. I've named her Teresa, after my late mother. I've sensed a growing discontent from Teresa about her current den.*
>
> *The progress on Teresa's new home in the South Central Animal Preserve is moving much more slowly than anticipated, but when the home is finished, it is almost certain to create an opportunity for everyone to study and appreciate animal life. It will also launch a restoration project of the entire preserve, an economic boon for all of South Central.*

Daniel closed the book and returned it to its place in his bag. He then pulled out a worn, spiral-bound sketchbook. The pencil art drawings had a fluid, graceful style. Some drawings were of various statues and mangled trees that he had found scattered throughout the districts. Others were of animals in the preserve: a rather large eagle that was known for its hostile nature, Teresa the lioness, and other smaller animals from various exhibits. Teresa was larger than one would expect, magnificent and healthy, unlike the other ailing animals that had long resided at the preserve.

Most of his drawings were faces of people he had surveyed during his hours of sketching practice, his attempts to capture their emotions on the page. Some drawings were accompanied by notes of what he imagined was in the hearts of his subjects.

"Is this all there is?"

"I can't go home until I find a way to solve this."

"He will never forgive me for this."

Some drawings went in a completely different direction: renderings of fantasy, of dragons and other mystical creatures from his vivid imagination. Daniel reached into the neck of his jacket and produced a silver griffin pendant. It hung from a dark-brown leather shoelace. He flipped it over to reveal an inscription that read "Da Il."

He clutched the miniature statue, and then tucked it back out of sight. This side of the park was less crowded, but passers-by acted the same; they seemed not to even notice that he was there. But he noticed them, and was always curious about what was going on inside, past the crestfallen gazes and outbursts of animosity.

He looked down at his book and flipped the page. On the left was a newspaper clipping entitled "Stay Above Ground." It had been released three years earlier to address a haunting rumor of an underground movement and the legend of Mr. Parker. As the story went, there was a man by the name of Joshua Parker. Mr. Parker had almost everything going for him: tall, dark, handsome, and confident, with a great job as a corporate executive. He had accomplished what most could not: a, title and position of success. That was difficult to do if you had not sworn allegiance to certain circles that were loyal to the Family. But the executive had hit a ceiling and began to feel trapped. Grinding day after day, he felt that the company line became a burden. He just got so tired of it all that, one day, he got up from his chair, stepped away from his cubicle, and simply left.

Sadly, no one really noticed at first. Perhaps the guards thought he was out for a late lunch, or to run an errand. Investigative leads confirmed that Mr. Parker had walked aimlessly for several blocks. He loosened the choking grip of his tie, removed his cufflinks, placing them in the pocket of his tailored gray slacks, and just kept walking. Then finally, after spotting one of the large grates built into the sidewalk, he lifted the heavy grill as a few looked on curiously. There, he descended into the tunnels, never to be heard from again.

Soon there were reports of other residents deciding not to follow the path predetermined for them, but making the choice to throw off the yoke and go underground. Most had too much to lose to make such a dramatic change, despite the well-accepted truth that a Commoner's life was a tough road, and it might be easier to just give in and pledge to join "the Family." This was regardless of the reality that the Family and its cult of followers were slowly draining the life out of Anthrazit. But residents there seemed under an inexplicable collective influence, strangely forgetful and apathetic. Ask those who knew Mr. Parker, and they were unable or unwilling to even describe what he looked like.

Daniel pulled out a pencil and began to make a quick sketch of the man he had seen at the entrance to the park. The drawing proved how sharp his memory was and how talented he was in his art form. The image bore a strong resemblance to the stranger and the burdened expression he displayed.

Cesar Blake was right about that. Anthrazit wasn't always this way, Daniel thought. He had heard a few reclusive older folks reminisce about the old days of making a good life for oneself and looking forward to putting down roots. Every now and then, there were tales, supposed sightings of magical creatures or something out of the ordinary spotted the night before. These rumors usually involved a location here or there in the massive underground tunnels under the city. Daniel himself thought that he had seen a shrub walking across the street one night when he was about six years old. Many of the statues on the older buildings seemed to have eyes that followed him, especially the gargoyle with massive wings that perched on top of the local parish church in South Central. These tales added a certain charm that used to make Anthrazit an enchanted and truly special place.

The small and remote city of Anthrazit was facing challenging economic times. After a three-year industrial boom two generations prior, the city's economy had hit a tailspin and had not recovered. Some called it the town that almost became a city. Making a living as a local merchant was the shared dream occupation of most residents. Tiny local shops were run by craftspeople and tradespersons fortunate enough to form small businesses around niche specialties.

The most beneficial work came from a corridor in the Industrial District. Merchant projects usually provided servicing and replacing of parts in a group of coal-power and food-engineering plants. The contracts for these projects were processed by the Financial District, which proved to be a tight gatekeeper on the flow of any capital or healthy commerce. This cultivated a grim culture in the city, which was predicated by a core belief that people should work as hard as they can for as long as they can, and maybe a gate would open.

Daniel closed his sketchbook and pulled something out of his bag. It was a map of the commonwealth, efficiently divided into four districts. Industrial and Financial were of equal size and sat on the west and east sides of the Central District, which was slightly larger. Clinging just below Central was a much smaller area, South Central. Daniel had previously highlighted the section of the transport path leading from South Central to the border of the Financial District.

The city was fenced in by a series of crisscrossing highways, many of which were falling apart at the columns. No one dared use them, with burdensome work and risky roadway exits, who traveled much, anyway? It had been generations since a traveler had come into Anthrazit, and no one Daniel knew had ever left. So they lived in a slowly decaying city, isolated and insular. A few impersonal edifices had been erected in the Central and Financial Districts and had been hailed as the beginnings of a new Anthrazit. But only one had been completed, and even it remained desolate and empty. Anthrazit had become a smog-filled trap, ruled by the damned.

Daniel pored over the map. The highways to the north formed a border against the desert wilderness, but of course each concrete column on these highways had been marked with the large, black squares that indicated they were structurally unsound and not safe for use. Failing highways to the south led to the Onyx Mountain Range, which was Anthrazit's only source of coal.

Beyond the industrial plants to the north was a vast expanse of dry wilderness, composed of red oxidized rock formations. Dust storms were frequent there—the huge plumes of dust clouds could be seen from the edges of the city. Only those who craved extreme adventure dared to go into the wilderness, and even those traveled at most a day's journey.

Daniel traced the path he had outlined with one finger. The transport's stop was actually at the opposite end of the park. He stood up and slung his bag over his shoulder, hoping he would make it in time.

CHAPTER 3
PROVIDENCE

When Daniel reached the other side of the park, he spotted the large, rumbling behemoth of a transport. It roared past and headed down the sloped street toward the stop at the next intersection, kicking up clouds of dust in its wake. He would have to pick up the pace if he wanted to make it on board.

The public transport had four wheels in front and four in back. Each wheel was a five-foot-wide, solid metal disc about two feet thick; the rims were wrapped in multiple concentric bands of rubber. Transports were coal-burning vehicles like the mobiles, but could carry masses with the three coal engines housed within the undercarriage. It was shaped like a wedge, with the bulk in the front, flanked by two rusted exhaust pipes that bellowed smoke. The back sloped down to a single bay door, attached at the top with bulky hinges. The paint was chipped and yellow, with a wide green stripe along the side. The words "Magic Transport" graced the side in scripted letters. Daniel's quick walk became a sprint as the transport came to a stop.

Large hydraulic spokes on the rear door lifted it open, releasing steam and soot. The passengers herded on board. The transport seated about forty passengers in rows on either side. For those who had planned ahead adequately, a seat was easily found, and settling in was a simple accomplishment. However, for those who were later in line, one of three poles lining the center of the transport, or hanging straps from the ceiling, were the only supports they would find. The transport became cramped very quickly.

Daniel leaped in and stumbled forward, knocking into the passengers ahead of him. A few straphangers got upset and responded to the accidental contact by pushing him into other passengers, who pushed him yet again. He was smaller in frame but bounced right back, quickly finding his footing.

"Sorry, pardon me," he responded in a soft voice. After steadying himself for a moment, he pulled down his scarf with his right hand and found a strap to hold for the commute.

With a big mechanical grunt, the eight-wheeled transport started on its way into the dusty, gray haze. Daniel leaned toward one of the small windows, looking out at the view—not that there was much to see. The dirt road soon gave way to a web of small highways, whose columns were marked with yellow squares, indicating that they were approved for transport usage, and the blue indicated approval for personal mobiles. The few vehicles on the roadway steered clear to avoid the Magic Transport and its fumes. The large transport picked up speed as it rattled along. They entered the highway entrance via an overpass and began to cruise control along. A second Magic Transport passed by, heading in the opposite direction.

"I'll find a way to get out of this place, and I'm never coming back!" said a spirited young voice.

Daniel glanced over as a father and son were having a loud, albeit private, conversation. The father was an imposing figure with pale skin, and he was wearing a long trench coat. The son's complexion was a warmer tone. The son made eye contact with Daniel as he stood on the opposite side of his father. The father became aware of Daniel and moved his frame to block Daniel's view as he continued to attempt to persuade his son in a more hushed tone.

Daniel Griffin needed no further clues; he had seen it all too many times before. Voices like that of the son didn't last long in the districts of Anthrazit. One day, a passionate youth is leading a movement; the next day, he or she is pledging. Just like their reasonable parents: pledge and get a job to put some food on the table.

"Just keep an open mind," the father replied.

The transport stopped at an intersection with a waiting booth. A few passengers exited. Some breathing room opened up, and everyone seemed to take a collective breath. The transport eased on once more, continuing its path toward Central District's southern border.

Daniel would have grown up in Central if he'd had a choice. There were more opportunities there, despite the heavy-handed control of the Vampire Family. South Central seemed to have gained a measure of freedom in exchange for a lack of resources. For some time, it had earned a moniker as "Anthrazit's Economic Cast off," among other not-so-pleasant nicknames. Magic Transport carved out a nice niche by providing a low-budget commute for South Central residents traveling in and out of other districts for work.

The transport made another stop, and Daniel was able to find a seat near the back. Two men shifted over next to him, still wrapped in quiet conversation.

"Where do you think he went?" one man asked the other.

"Anywhere! Imagine if you were prime minister," the second man replied.

Daniel often wondered the same. One day, Prime Minister Latimus Drake sat down with his most-trusted advisors, and his appointed priest, Aitalas, and drafted a canon. The ruling blueprint outlined every matter, providing regulations for resolving disputes, duties to be performed, and even how many brides or husbands each of his direct descendants was allowed to have. For each district, Minister Drake placed five of his true blood descendants as ruling governors. South Central was the exception, since no descendant or advisor saw any value in it. With fifteen descendants in ruling positions, and about twenty others left to run the primary programs and matters of the small city, the minister made his departure. Although not a true blood descendant, the priest Aitalas was granted final oversight and veto power on certain matters.

Then the prime minister went away on a long trip, citing an economic summit in a faraway city. He amassed an entourage of one hundred members, which included high-ranking true blood descendants, vampires in various assistant roles, and a number of Commoners chosen by a lottery. Some considered his trip a brave move to secure an economic future for Anthrazit, but the lengthy absence began to draw doubt. Some considered it a long hiatus in his rule. Still others speculated it was a trip meant to seek out a new adventure, leaving his descendants holding the bag.

A uniformed police officer walked through the transport, surveying the passengers. He stopped in front of Daniel.

"Let's see your registration card," said the officer as he commenced profiling duties. Daniel searched his bag and handed his card to the waiting officer. "Daniel Griffin, what's your business today?"

"I don't have one…well, kind of. I'm an artist, and—" Daniel began to explain.

The officer shoved the card back at Daniel and made his way around a few standing passengers, continuing his rounds. Daniel was great at observing and studying others, but lacked self-confidence. His trip into Central was supposed to be the start of changing that, but since he couldn't stand the sight of someone else's blood, much less his own, his elaborate scheme was falling apart.

When Daniel got wind of the news that the young, brilliant zoologist, Jessica Winters, was running a contest to find the best artist in Anthrazit, he became obsessed with improving his talent and learning as much as he could about her. The chosen artist would become the chief artistic director of the South Central Animal Preserve, creating an extensive series of murals to bring new life to the landmark institution. This was Daniel's one shot at a career doing something he truly loved, making a decent living, and skipping the pledge to the ruling Family cult. Given the odds—one poor, self-taught artist facing off against an army of trained art students—there were a lot of reasons for doubt. A small inner voice told Daniel that perhaps this was more of a wild chase, but Daniel had little to lose.

The encounter with the officer had rattled Daniel, and he thought a quick sketch would calm his nerves. He pulled out his sketchbook and glanced around for a subject.

Then he saw her. It was only the back of her head, but he could recognize Ms. Winters, even so. Her dark hair was held neatly in place with a wooden barrette and a gold-plated dowel. His heart began to pound, and his hands began to tremble. His palms were slick with sweat.

She sat completely motionless in the first passenger seat at the front of the transport, not looking up or down, to the right side or the left, just straight ahead, almost right into the future. Perhaps it was the haze as it reflected through the front windshield, but she seemed to have a glowing aura of serenity. She was statuesque at the head of this vessel upon which Daniel found himself traveling.

"Her picture does not do her justice," Daniel thought. Entranced by the sight of her, he began his drawing. The Magic Transport made more stops. Passengers would exit at the front as they were required to do, they would board from the back, and, from time to time, they would block Daniel's view. As soon as they shifted out of the way, he would add to the drawing in progress.

Jessica Winters moved, almost ruining the perspective the young man had going. But it was glorious to see that she was a living, breathing person. In one elegant motion, she placed her hand at the base of her neck and swept her hair back. Her head turned just enough for him to catch a glimpse of the side of her high cheekbones, flawless neckline, and the frame of her glasses. She was such a contrast to the dull figures that surrounded her, seemingly taking whatever light there was and reflecting it brighter.

The transport ride became bumpy, but Daniel was undeterred. Despite potholes, bumps, sudden brakes, or gearshifts, come what may, he steadily applied his skill to capturing his vision.

Soon an obtuse man standing close took notice and peered down at the sketchpad. He looked over at the unsuspecting young woman, then down at the sketch, then back and forth a few more times, and finally made the connection. "Hey, that's pretty good!" he announced loudly so the whole transport could hear. Daniel cringed.

She looked over. Her face was more beautiful than he had imagined. Their eyes met for the longest three seconds of Daniel's life. Though he sat at the back of the transport, it was as if they were face to face. Daniel turned away, barely acknowledging the compliment from the man. The Magic Transport came to a stop, and Jessica rose to her feet. The doors opened before her. Daniel looked up, but she was gone.

He sat dumbfounded for some time. "What were the odds that I would be riding on the same transport as Jessica Winters, and why didn't she have her own mobile?," he wondered. But as the transport made its way into the most dilapidated section of South Central, it wasn't long before his gloomy, everyday reality returned. Daniel peered through the small window.

Many buildings sat like crumbling, hollowed-out carcasses. This is where, years before, it had happened—the first and only rebellion against the governing Family. The ruins remained as a monument to anyone who dared to cross them. The retaliation was quick and ruthless. Not only did the Family march in with law enforcement on their side, but they also used specially trained vampire assassins to infiltrate and strike down targets even as the rebels retreated to the edges of South Central. Whatever their true cause was for bravery had utterly failed. There was a large piece of graffiti on the side of a building that read, "Magic is real!" The battle cry of the rebellion.

As the building faded into the distance, Daniel was reminded of how the naming of Magic Transport system was a shrewd capitalization on those hopes and dreams.

The transit reached its final stop; the driver pulled up and began powering down the coal engines. Daniel sunk into his seat, hoping not to get noticed, and it became clear that he had no place to be. Eventually, the driver looked into a small mirror and noticed him.

"Young man, you don't have to go home, but you can't stay here," he remarked.

Daniel hung his head and shuffled to the front exit. He hesitated and looked at the driver, who had begun making copious notes into a ledger. He was a rotund older man, pushing his uniform to its limits. The company logo with three stars was embroidered on the shirt pocket. He had a bald head and a gray beard covering his mouth, which masked his words as he spoke.

"What are you waiting for? A transport is not a shelter for strays. Now get," the old driver rebuked, yet he had a strange glint in his eye.

Despite a humble and sympathetic look on Daniel's face, the driver didn't change his mind. He disembarked, standing on the dusty road and watching as the transport rumbled away.

The driver reminded Daniel of Father Frank. He was a stern, overprotective man, not given to much display of affection. For most of his life, Daniel convinced himself that just having a roof over his head was enough. Even at the age of eight, Daniel was acutely aware that a place to call home wasn't something every kid was lucky enough to have.

He was well fed, though his guardian, Father Frank, didn't understand why a kid would willingly choose not to eat meat of any kind. Out of frustration one day, witnessing Daniel's lack of decent muscle tone, he attempted to force the ten-year-old to eat some GMO meat, which was the primary source of protein for the disadvantaged, unturned population. Daniel became violently ill, suffering from seizures, chills, and high fever for days. Daniel became bedridden, and it appeared that Father Frank was about to lose the boy.

On the seventh day, Father Frank was forced to acknowledge that his home remedies had failed. He brought in a local pharmacist to visit Daniel's bedside in the barely lit room. The boy lay pale and drenched in sweat, his eyes glazed over and only slightly open.

The pharmacist was an abnormally tall fellow—even now, Daniel could remember. He'd worn a large-collared shirt and dark-brown pants held up by suspenders, topped by a navy-blue lab coat. His face was a dark shadow. He touched Daniel's temples, and something about the fingers beneath the man's blue latex gloves made Daniel's skin itch.

"I've seen cases of food poisoning, but this is by far the worst. Poor kid," said the pharmacist. He sat at the edge of the bed, and wiped Daniel's forehead with a cool, moist towel. Daniel began to wheeze, gasping for breath. "But you are a fighter, aren't you?"

"Dr. Bol, maybe I should take him into Grace Central. If you think that's best," Father Frank said reluctantly.

The pharmacist wrapped his fingers around the pendant on Daniel's neck and suddenly chuckled. He clasped his hands in front of his mouth prayerfully.

"Please, just call me Mr. Bol; a doctor's license is beyond me, I'm afraid," the pharmacist replied. "However, that hospital visit might not be necessary just yet."

He pulled a dark-brown medicine bottle from his black leather medicine bag, reached in, and drew out a large metal spoon. Mr. Bol opened the bottle and began pouring a thick, viscous liquid onto the spoon. He lifted Daniel's head and inserted the spoon into his mouth. Daniel reacted to spit out the bitter, goopy substance, but Mr. Bol held his mouth shut and clutched him close to his chest with the other hand. Daniel began to kick and twist, but Mr. Bol wouldn't let go.

"What are you doing?" Father Frank screamed.

"It's root-mulch molasses, a special herbal remedy. Made the batch myself. Just give it a minute," Mr. Bol replied and then began to whisper in Daniel's ear. The words were inaudible to Father Frank, but still they sank deep into Daniel's heart. "You are cursed, yet you live. You are stronger than we thought. Just relax. I'm not trying to hurt you."

Daniel calmed, and the pharmacist rested the boy's head on the pillow. Daniel was still faint but more alert than he'd been in a long time. Mr. Bol leaned in and kissed him on the forehead. He then sealed the bottle and placed it along with the spoon into his bag and stood to leave. Daniel noticed that the pharmacist's glove on his right hand had ripped in the struggle, and what appeared to be leaves were sticking out. The pharmacist quickly placed the hand in the pocket of his lab coat and began to exit the room, and with a finger over his lips, he gestured for Daniel to remain quiet.

"How did you know that was going to work?" questioned the father.

"I didn't. That stuff isn't really meant for...certain people. Just go easy on him for a little while, okay?"

"Thank you," Father Frank said.

Mr. Bol gave Father Frank an awkward left-hand shake and departed.

Father Frank kept Daniel on bed rest for a few more days, but he was clearly on the mend. He gave Daniel a large notepad to keep him busy, and that notepad became Daniel's first sketchbook. He then bought the boy a secondhand guitar. Daniel liked it okay but preferred drawing.

Father Frank came in one afternoon to check on Daniel and found him sitting beside a small table. He took note of Daniel's drawings.

"Not bad," said Father Frank. "As a matter of fact, I think I have a little project for you."

"Okay," replied Daniel. "Do I have to eat that stuff again?"

"No, never again," answered the father repentantly.

"Father Frank, do you think one day I can find my parents?"

"Leave you alone for a little while, and your thoughts go wandering off to who knows where," the father answered.

He knelt at the side of a little table where Daniel sat. "Do you remember what I told you about finding you in the arms of that statue?"

Daniel nodded in response.

"Let's leave it there. No good could come from such a search. Now let's talk about this mural project I have in mind for the church."

By early afternoon, Daniel's thoughts found their way back to Jessica. He tried to discern if he should attend the ceremony only in hopes of seeing her in person again.

"The feverish influence she has on my senses can't be a good thing," Daniel said to himself as he walked along the edge of the empty dam. He jumped over a low, rusted fence, parted the thickets, and made his way down the steep incline.

With a few hours before the drink ceremony, he debated with himself as to how to justify why he chose to go to a drink ceremony, one of the few things Father Frank instructed him never to do.

Daniel wasn't always beholden to the way he was raised. As an orphan, he was grateful for someone taking him in at a young enough age before forming any memories of living on the street, but he did have this streak about him, a compelling drive to make it on his own terms.

"So many rules," he now thought. Come right home after school; don't hang out with vampires. At some point I need to make my own choices, right?" he argued with his conscience. "Not that I would choose to do those things, at least not without a good reason. I'm strong enough, and I can handle it. That's right; I'm going."

He crossed the bottom of the dam and clambered into a large concrete tube. Daniel kept his head bowed as he made his way through until the tube ended in a closed metal hatch, blocked by broken wooden beams. Daniel moved the beams aside and pushed against the hatch, but it wouldn't budge. He shouldered into the door as hard as he could, and he fell in, hitting his shin against the metal frame of an old cot. Daniel grimaced in pain. He closed the hatch, and took a seat on the bed, holding his injured leg.

This was an unused sewer connection joint, which was now serving an entirely different purpose as Daniel's temporary home. The concrete enclosure was eight feet tall and about two hundred square feet with a hatch on each of its four walls, some larger than others. On his previous visits, Daniel had placed an assortment of his belongings in each corner.

An earlier theory that he would find the underground Commoners had proved misguided, and Daniel had spent days stumbling around in the tunnels. That was how he had first found this place. Accidentally finding this enclosure had been something just short of a miracle. Now, he was on his own again, with only a few bills to his name and without adequate shelter.

Daniel scooted over to a large, overly ornate yellow dresser. It was sure to have been the belle of its day, but now it was severely battered, and chipped on all corners. A cement block served to support two missing legs. He opened a drawer and retrieved a plastic bag he had collected on a recent scavenger trip to a motel. Daniel turned the bag upside down in midair above the bed. A bar of soap, a thin mint-green toothbrush, and a miniature tube of toothpaste rained down from within the bag.

He took off his beanie cap and ruffled his brownish-blond hair with his right hand and then scratched at the back of his right ear rapidly, wiggling his nose in a pensive manner. He then used both hands and picked up an oval mirror that was once part of the dresser, placing it where it was once stationed. Daniel stood up and peered into the mirror. There was a grate at one corner of the ceiling, but Daniel had cleverly sealed it from outside with a tarp.

The lighting was dim, but just bright enough to make out the idiosyncratic features that made Daniel stand out, for better or worse. He protruded his jaw, revealing lower canine teeth slightly larger than average, and then closed his mouth to conceal them again. He shifted back his scruffy, unruly hair to reveal a pair of ears seemingly ordinary in every other manner, but that for some reason came to a point at the top. This is the reason he wore that hat and his hair at that strange length; it was just enough to cover up this oddity.

"Why would a perfectly decent pair of ears do that?" Daniel wondered aloud.

He used his fingers to comb his hair over his ears once more. Resting his arms on the top of the dresser, he leaned forward, almost nose to nose with his reflection.

He had subtle freckles on his cheeks, and his eyelids were pink and watery, as if he were constantly fighting some allergy.

Then the one thing that made him the most self-conscious came into focus. Daniel had heterochromia: one iris was blue and the other hazel. Two separate eye colors can be caused by trauma to the eyes or, as in his case, a genetic condition. Daniel had two separate eye colors from birth. It was something that most people reacted to negatively if they ever got close enough to notice, so Daniel avoided direct eye contact at all times. As he continued to gaze into his own eyes, something caught his attention.

"Just great," he said with a sigh.

Growing among the freckles on the right side of his mouth was a single long hair, and it hung pronounced like a long yellow whisker. He marched away from the mirror and then returned. It was still there. He looked away and back again. It was now so blatant that it was the only thing he could see.

Daniel began to peel off the layers of his clothing. After removing three layers of outerwear, he was left in a thin white t-shirt. Daniel was beyond just being lanky; there was barely enough fat on his body to fill a teaspoon. He reached over to the bed, grabbed the toiletries, and headed for the hatch on the left wall.

He opened the heavily bolted hatch. To be cautious, he peered out slowly. The coast was clear, and he emerged from the small opening under an abandoned bridge overpass. Fresh water rushed along the floor of this inlet to the dam. Daniel grabbed a red bucket, scooped in the fresh water, and retuned inside, closing the hatch behind him. He took a small metal cup and filled it with a little water and began to brush his teeth. Soon, white foam from the toothpaste covered his mouth as he continued to scrub side to side. He looked in the mirror one more time. Yep, the lone hair was still there, mocking him.

Daniel finished up and discarded the waste down a capped tube on the other side of the space. He returned to the mirror, ready to reengage the whisker, fully prepared to do what he had decided was necessary. Daniel wrapped the stringy hair around his index finger and yanked it out by the root.

"Ah!" he screamed as a little blood started to dot his cheek.

He placed a finger on the throbbing area and scrambled with his other hand to open the drawer to find a bandage. No luck. Daniel tore a piece of tissue to help clot the wound. The white tissue stuck on with a bright round spot of blood showing through.

He sat on the edge of the bed as a calmer, more rational inner voice began to speak to him. Jessica Winters is a girl—no, a woman—who you've never met, and never spoken to. What has come over you, Daniel? This is not even a date. All this might be okay if it was a date. But it's not."

He pulled out his sketchbook, turned to the page where he had made his incomplete sketch of Jessica Winters, and sat silently as he pondered. *"It's not too late to change your mind,"* he thought, *"and no one will know you came up with this silly idea."*

He reached over and pulled out the brochure that Cesar had given him; it shined even in the dim light. It was titled "Family Is Everything." Daniel had to admit that there was a tug on his heartstrings, since he grew up as an orphan. The brochure folded out in many panels, showing happy singles and couples with their kids. The panels were subdivided into areas of red and black with white type. He read thoroughly as it laid out answers to commonly asked questions:

What is a true- blood family member?

These are family members that are direct descendants of Prime Minister Drake. Like any family, they enjoy life here in Anthrazit and do the best they can for the city's health and wellbeing.

What is a drink ceremony?

These are private gatherings, where what we call adopted Drake Family and close friends meet to celebrate the life and vitality that being a vampire brings. Along with a typical meal such as any normal group of friends would share, willing pledges will offer their blood to attending vampires to drink freely, and in exchange are accepted as adopted members of the vampire community. If the pledge has completed an aptitude test in advance, he or she will be dedicated to a leadership track as a part of the ceremony. The blessing of the vampire bloodline will be bestowed upon the pledge by a ruling elder in attendance.

What are the benefits of pledging?

All pledges are encouraged to take an aptitude test. This test helps us to get a sense of your physical and intellectual strengths. All of these traits will be heightened when the blessing of the vampire bloodline is received. Each accepted pledge is automatically fast-tracked to his or her most suitable position in the region of Anthrazit, where the Family has significant networks and relationships. No pledge who has passed the test and joined the Family will ever go in want. Some do offer themselves to refresh vampires without pledging, and we are truly thankful.

What are the risks?

Certainly nothing worth gaining in life comes without risk. Not every pledge has a strong enough blood type or genetic makeup to survive the transition into vampirism.

Some risk factors include loss of higher brain functions or physical deformity. These risks are rare. Please speak to one of our licensed doctors to find out if pledging is the right choice for you.

What is a Nosferatu?
Joining the Family is all about becoming a better you, providing heightened strength, intelligence, and satisfaction beyond your wildest dreams. Occasionally we meet someone who is truly exceptional, a candidate that has all the makings of someone already extremely gifted, and he or she is willing to pledge above and beyond, devoting his or her entire self to the vampire way of life. These pledges voluntarily trade their physical beauty and wealth for a life of service and devotion, allowing vampires to feast upon both their blood and flesh. In return, they inherit the supernatural, including being able to walk through objects, speed, strength, and, most of all, a share in the hearts and minds of the true blood Family. This utter devotion is not for everyone; we encourage you to speak with a Nosferatu inductee and your doctor to learn more.

"Well, this is all a lie," Daniel muttered. He had been taught better. The pamphlet conveniently kept silent on the fact that the Nosferatu were also shape-shifters, and so they worked as spies for the Vampire Family. Daniel knew enough not to be tempted by the offerings in the glossy brochure, but a chilling thought crossed his mind. What if Jessica Winters was planning to pledge?

"Oh, that would suck," he said aloud in horror and then cringed at his choice of words. He stood up, still seized by the thought of it. "You should go save her!" he commanded his image in the mirror, as he pointed a finger. "At least make sure she isn't planning on drinking anybody...or that nobody is planning on drinking her."

Daniel inflated his chest a bit, grabbed his shirt, sweater, and outer jacket, and got dressed in a hurry.

CHAPTER 4
THE MASQUERADE

Daniel arrived fashionably late, when the faint light of day had already started to fade. He stood on the sidewalk a good distance from the house, considering a last-minute change of mind. A small itch on his cheek reminded him that he still had a little patch of tissue paper there. He brushed it away quickly.

The house was a small mansion: a freestanding, three-story home with a wide lawn all around. The lawn was bordered by a knee-high, white picket fence with a small gate at the front entrance and a tall, ivy-covered fence in the back. The path from the gate parted a perfectly manicured lawn about forty feet from the porch that wrapped around the house. Tiny paper lanterns were strung along the beams of the porch, each holding captive a small amber light that flickered through the cobalt-shaded smog.

Daniel could hear the sound of loud guitars and drums, cutting and kicking their way through the air from inside. The festivities were well under way, and a few attendants mingled on the porch. Everyone seemed well dressed. Daniel stood motionless, holding, the business card of the banker who'd invited him, all the while blocking the flow of traffic through the gate. A giddy couple knocked him forward off his heels.

"Pardon me," the well-dressed young man apologized.

The socialite commoner wore a dark blazer, a light-blue shirt, and khaki pants. The young lady on his arm wore a fitted black silk cocktail dress. She turned her head, tossing her long, wavy brown hair and giving Daniel a flirtatious smile. Her lips were dressed in rouge and tipped with a seductive pair of fangs. Daniel gulped as the couple continued down the path.

Daniel was glaringly underdressed for this event. "Just act confident. Maybe they'll think you're part of the band," he said to bolster his confidence as he began to saunter down the path.

He slipped the card into his pocket and tried to loosen up. Then he added a little swagger. A couple of guys hanging out on the lawn waved in his direction, and he waved back just before realizing they meant the greeting for another group on the opposite side. His confidence fell flat just before he hit the porch. Daniel made his way up the five short steps onto the patio.

On the left were two women swinging slightly on a hanging bench. "Good evening, ladies," attempted Daniel with a veneer of machismo. They both looked away, and one whispered in the other's ear.

As Daniel moved to the doorframe, a large man stepped out from the interior. He was wide enough to fill the entire door, and just as tall; Daniel thought he could walk beneath the man's armpit without stooping. The giant looked down at Daniel. "Is your name on the list?" he asked in a deep, monotone voice, his eyes glazed over and his pupils almost as white as his eyeballs.

"I'm with the band?" Daniel replied, framing his response more like a question. There was no response. "Just kidding. I was invited..." Daniel glanced down at his hand, wondering where that business card had gone to.

"Oh, Daniel, there you are. Come in." It was Cesar in a charcoal-gray suit.

The bouncer barely moved to allow Daniel to enter.

The banker gave him a hearty handshake and threw his left arm over Daniel's shoulder. "Glad you could make it. Listen, get a drink, make yourself comfortable, and we'll chat later." Cesar was already tipsy, whether from alcohol or blood. "Hey, if you decide to pledge, tell me first, okay? I want those bonus points, all right?" He winked and then motioned to the two young ladies.

"Sure," Daniel replied.

Cesar took one lady on each arm and disappeared into the large hall, which was overcrowded with bobbing and uncoordinated silhouetted figures. Beyond, he could see that the front of the room was outfitted with a bar, where scores of liquor bottles acted as prisms for cool blue neon lights. It was a nice contrast to the warm yellow glow provided by several candles stationed on ledges and windowsills throughout the first floor.

Daniel stayed in the narrow hallway just for a moment. The living room was a no-go, even if he wanted to. There was a narrow, wooden, winding staircase that headed upstairs, and straight ahead was a small room central to the house, where the band was playing on a temporary stage.

Choosing the path of least bodily resistance, Daniel headed toward the stage. The bandleader's mouth was buried in the microphone, but his words became clearer as Daniel approached. Although most people were in anything from casual dress to cocktail-party attire, some wore elaborate costumes or sported glittery masquerade masks of various colors and with different types of feathers.

A young woman caught his eye. Her purple sequined mask sparkled in the warm yellow candlelight, and its dark feathers waved softly. She brought down her mask to reveal an utterly mangled face. Daniel gasped in horror. She swiped the mask in front of her face, bringing it down again to reveal a beautiful young woman's face without a spot or blemish. She was a Nosferatu; she brushed up against him as she passed by.

"We are going to make this drink ceremony go EP!" the bandleader's voice boomed, jolting Daniel out of his daze. The crowd cheered as the band's vocalist continued. "As y'all know, tonight is a special night." He paused, strumming a few chords on the guitar that hung from his neck. "Thanks to the generosity of the Hawthorne family. Let's give a special welcome to Leonardo, as the first official governor of South Central." The audience applauded. "That's right, give it up for him," the bandleader encouraged.

Daniel made his way to the front of the crowd, until he could see beyond the blinding spotlights. The band had five members. The bandleader wore a button-down suit vest and a long-sleeved white shirt. He also wore a narrow brimmed hat, which was pulled down, covering much of his face, but it was not enough to hide a deformed appearance. The skin of his face seemed to sag; its tone wasn't pale but still appeared to be not completely normal.

"Now some might ask why Leonardo wants to be governor of SC. Wasn't he the one in charge of turning it into a dump?" he continued. "My theory? Nature is calling, and he's here to make a deposit." He delivered his punch line to a smattering of loud laughter and several boos. The bandleader shrugged and laughed. "No, but seriously, congrats to the new gov. Where is that son of a bitch?" That joke also met mixed reviews but more laughter this time. "Governor Leonardo is picking out his little harem today. Whoot!" he hollered into the microphone, and the guests cheered loudly. "That's right! So, ladies, hold that neck out. It could be your lucky night."

With that, the bandleader turned to his band mates, kicking them off on an up-tempo beat.

Out of the corner of his eye, to the left front area of the stage, Daniel spotted Jessica Winters perched on a bar stool next to a high, round table. Next to her stood a man with gray hair dressed in a white suit. He was Mr. Lance Hawthorne III, a board member of the Animal Preserve, host of the gathering, and Ms. Winters' personal advisor, whether she wanted it or not. His lips were moving rapidly at her ear, and while she nodded periodically with the pretense that she was listening, her eyes traveled the room, flickering and bored. Her hair was swept into a two-tiered bulb, with the wooden barrette now propped up in front and two dowels piercing the top of the bun. She wore a form-fitting, sleeveless red dress that accentuated her gorgeously long neck and showcased her elegant arms. She held a martini glass in her right hand.

Daniel straightened his collar as he strode toward her. He gripped the strapped bag with his bare hand. Jessica's lips began to move, but Daniel could not hear what she was saying. He was stunned at hearing her speak for the first time. His imagination scurried about as he tried to find an apt comparison for the sound of her voice.

Mr. Hawthorne glanced down at Daniel. "Oh, God, not another wide-eyed admirer," he said and made a dismissive gesture.

She ignored him. "Are you an artist?" she repeated as Daniel craned his neck forward. Her voice was like water filling a glass, a low, full tone with accenting crescendos.

Daniel nodded vigorously, and in his smile he caught the scent of her, like freshly cut carnations. His head spun.

Jessica grabbed him by the elbow and led him through the crowd.

"You shouldn't talk to him. If you do, he's disqualified," Mr. Hawthorne yelled.

Jessica led Daniel up the winding staircase and onto the second floor. He glanced back just as the new governor, Leonardo, emerged onto the landing below from a staircase that plunged down to lower levels. For a moment, he and Daniel locked gazes.

Leonardo was sharply dressed in a custom-tailored tuxedo suit, his blond hair slicked back. He narrowed his chiseled brow at Daniel, but when three women approached him and clung to his shoulders, starving for affection, he glanced down with a smirk. Aitalas stepped up to Leonardo as well, dressed in dark, flowing priestly robes. He tapped Leonardo on the shoulder; the new governor brushed off the clinging women, and the two began to walk toward the stage.

"Come on," Jessica hissed, and Daniel followed after.

They walked down a narrow hallway, past a guest who smiled at Jessica and then blinked confusedly at Daniel. Further down the hallway, they squeezed past a couple that seemed to have had trouble finding a room. Daniel dared not analyze whether their impassioned display was of the vampire or natural variety.

"Where are we going?" he whispered.

"I don't know."

Right then, they came upon a set of glass French doors. The light from the hallway seeped before them to reveal wood paneling and inset bookshelves. Jessica grabbed the gold-plated handles and jostled them, but the doors wouldn't open. She gave them a slight bump with her hip, and they gave way gently. She pulled him in and closed the door behind them.

In the room were two high-backed, coffee-colored leather chairs. Jessica sat in one and reclined with her knees meeting and her ankles apart. Daniel sat in the other chair just as a passing couple looked in through the doors, regretfully eyeing the romantic setting.

Jessica slowly began to compose herself; she sat up straight, crossing her long, beautiful legs to the side, and then placed two fingers at the temple of her forehead. Daniel's shifting produced squeaking sounds from the friction against the leather. The hum of the band buzzed in the floor.

"I'm so sorry," said Jessica. "I just had to get out of there." She looked at Daniel, who was looking at the floor and wiping his sweaty palms along the side of his pants. "He's right, you know. If you had any hopes of entering that contest, I've ruined your application."

"It's okay. I can't afford the entry fee anyway," Daniel replied as he kept his gaze downward.

"I should look at your work. When I saw your bag, I knew you were an artist. Who else would carry such a thing? If you have some work, I would really like to see it. It's the least I could do," Jessica offered.

⸺⸱⸱⸺

The night's festivities were approaching the main event, and everyone crammed together along the floor space. The hardwood floor shifted to reveal a recessed area, three steps down with a floor of stone. Leonardo sat in a large, elaborately carved chair at the head of the pit, checking his watch obsessively. The priest was pacing at the opposite end.

In the pit, Cesar was hunched over another man, latched onto his neck. "Drink, drink, drink," the guests chanted. The banker stood and threw his head back in a moment of euphoria, shoving the man to the side. The crowd cheered as a middle-aged man ran to the aid of the pledge. If Daniel had been there, he would have recognized them; they were the father and son who had been arguing on the transport earlier that day.

"How do you feel?" he asked as he grabbed his son's elbow and escorted him to the edge of the pit.

"I'm good," the son replied, still faint and disoriented from the ordeal. His eyes darkened, and his skin started to become pale and cold.

"He's good," exclaimed the father. He raised his hand and pumped his fist.

"Welcome to the Family," the crowd shouted in unison and applauded.

Leonardo checked his watch again.

Priest Aitalas had a very old, wrinkly face with red eyes. On his head sat a tall, dark cap; his hands were covered in black gloves all the way up to his elbows. Every move he made carried a dark, ominous, magical quality. Many referred to him as the "dark priest," and he didn't mind the label.

He shifted his garments, moved a few steps, and then reached for a ledge behind to pick up a long staff. The head of the staff was fitted with wrought-iron prongs at the top, which held a faceted ruby about the size of a fist.

Aitalas raised the staff, and the room became quiet. "And the moment we've all been waiting for," he said. His words commanded a cheer, but the tone of his voice was foreboding. "The choosing of the brides of Governor Leonardo."

They applauded loudly, but only until the dark priest exalted the staff once more.

"All unattached ladies, come," he pronounced.

The crowd began to shuffle as a line of beautiful women stepped forward.

The young couple that had bumped Daniel on their way through the front gate stood at the side. To the man's surprise, his young female companion left him to join the line. He grabbed her hand. "Please, don't do this," he begged in a hushed voice, not wanting to make a scene.

She raised her left hand, dangling her empty ring finger—proof that he had no cause to claim her as his own.

"Any woman can seek to be a governor's wife during his season of choosing," the priest added as the line grew and grew. "It doesn't matter if you are turned or pledging for the first time, although the youngest child here has been known to like the taste of something fresh. Isn't that right, Leonardo?" Aitalas taunted.

The line of potential brides-to-be marched into the pit and began to form neat rows. Some were jittery, worried that their back-row position would diminish their chances. They stood on tiptoes to increase their visibility.

"Space is limited for what might be the last chance of a lifetime," coached the priest as Leonardo looked out over the herd of women. He slightly eased himself out of the chair by the elbows to see the back rows, searching.

"Daniel, these are amazing," Jessica exclaimed as she leaned over the drawings, studying each page.

She placed a finger at the edge of her lips, gently biting on it as she marveled. Her teeth weren't perfect, but she didn't have fangs, Daniel was relieved to notice.

"I've been to the parish in South Central," Jessica continued in an excited tone as she looked at his study drawings for the mural. "You did that? I love that mural."

Daniel kept his gaze on her. "Thank you," he said politely.

She looked up. Their heads were so close, they almost bumped foreheads. Daniel looked away out of a conditioned response.

"I've read your book," he said. He pulled the powder-blue, dog-eared book from his bag, opened it, and showed her where he had underlined passages as he continued to gush over her, lavishing compliments.

"I love animals, all kinds, but especially felines. They are so majestic and breathtaking," she admitted. "We're killing them, slowly but surely. Teresa is the first I've found that proves my childhood accounts. That old bird is no fluke—there are larger, more dominant species subsets living beyond Anthrazit. Teresa is all that, but also has an incredibly gentle spirit about her."

"So I bet finding the lioness was a really big deal. Sorry, I feel like I'm just repeating stuff you already described scientifically and beautifully in your book. And just now…, you said it really beautifully, just now." Daniel rambled.

Jessica looked at him curiously and smiled.

"Naming her after your late mother was very touching."

Jessica's cheeks puffed as if to restrain herself from saying something. She looked away.

"It probably makes the memory of your parents more present," Daniel continued, wanting to prove his sincerity. "I'm an orphan, too, and we need something that helps us reconnect with what we've lost." He held his pendant in his hand and began to look at it.

"It seems we have an awful lot in common, don't we? Losing parents, and having to grow up much faster than anyone should have to," said Jessica, and her shoulders relaxed ever so slightly.

Time slipped away as the two talked and shared both serious and silly stories from their pasts.

"There's got to be a way to work around this little snafu. You aren't the only applicant I've met. S-CAP could really use murals done by an artist with such a love for animals, a great imagination, and talent," said Jessica.

"I still can't afford it," Daniel replied; he wanted to make eye contact but couldn't bring himself to do so.

Jessica placed her hand on his shoulder. "If you really want this, you'll find a way. I'll do what I can, but you must also do your part." She looked down at a slender watch on her left wrist, and her eyes widened. She paused with her lips still slightly parted, as her joyous mood began to fade. "I should go."

Jessica stood up and headed for the doors. Before the words even formed in his mind, Daniel blurted out, "Don't get drunk tonight!"

⟞⟞ ⟝⟝

Downstairs, Leonardo was almost having the time of his life. The newly appointed governor had already drunk from twenty women, and found it difficult to select the remaining few for his harem.

"How many more do I have?" asked Leonardo. He rested his elbows on his quads, but they kept slipping. He leaned forward on the edge of his temporary throne. His unmade bowtie hung loosely from the collar of his well-pressed white shirt, which was now stained with blood from multiple contributors. Leonardo rocked from side to side. "How many?"

"Six more," Cesar answered, clapping boisterously. He tapped Leonardo on the shoulder to egg him on.

"Don't forget, I'm saving a spot," Leonardo slurred.

The banker failed to accurately account for the women already chosen. Leonardo was allowed twenty-five, and Cesar only counted nineteen, missing the previously turned young woman with the wavy brown hair.

The selected brides stood and clapped, bravely nursing the punctures on their necks, all except the woman with the long brown hair, who sat dejected on the floor. Leonardo hadn't even cared to bite within the puncture holes she already had. He bit her ravenously and left her with an even bigger gaping pair of bite marks just above the previous entry points. Then he tossed her to the side, another unwanted trophy.

"Choose wisely," advised the priest, who sat on the side watching, keeping tally in a small notepad. This coming-of-age party for a true blood was far less dignified or discrete than the affairs he usually oversaw, but it had its place, he supposed.

A line of women hoping to be chosen strutted down toward the young governor and then turned to the right or the left, circling to the back of the line.

"Get that one. Damn, she is hot! Get that one, too," instigated Cesar.

Leonardo raised his left hand and snapped his fingers to summon the two women. They both ran up, eager and giddy. They kneeled one in front of the other before Leonardo; he grabbed the first by the back of the neck with both hands and leaned in. He opened his mouth to reveal elaborately engraved gold-plated fangs. Leonardo bit into her, and her eyes opened widely, shocked at the force with which he drew her blood and the acidic burn that began from the puncture wound and radiated throughout her body. She began to shiver, and Leonardo tossed her aside and went on to the next. With a slight roll, she clambered to her feet, aided by two other brides while the others clapped. The young woman flashed a bright, fake smile as she reached over her neck to touch the tender, throbbing wounds, pressing on them gently to aid in the clotting.

<hr />

"Don't get drunk. I don't mean drinking…well, that, too, but don't join the blood-drink ceremony," Daniel continued, stumbling over his words.

Jessica looked over her shoulder at the nervous boy. His griffin pendant was now on the outside of his shirt.

"It was a pleasure meeting you," she replied gently with an air of resignation. "Be well."

As she quietly descended the staircase, there was a loud roar from the crowd. She spotted Leonardo holding his right fist in the air and making galloping prances, falling onto onlookers in the front row. He had taken his jacket off and thrown it on the arm of the chair. The sleeves of his shirt were rolled up to just above his elbows. He stumbled in his stupor, almost as if he caught the scent of Jessica. He turned and wiped the blood from his mouth.

"Perfect timing," he mumbled, as he began to make his way to the other side of the recessed floor with quick, uncoordinated steps.

The ruby on Priest Aitalas's staff began to glow a bright red. The priest rose to his feet, scanning the room. While the crowd cheered, the bandleader watched from his raised platform behind the brides. He looked up from under the brim of his hat and motioned for his band mates to stay put. He then removed his string instrument from his shoulder and, broke the neck of the instrument, pulling out a long, silver dagger and hiding the weapon behind his back. He pushed through the cluster of brides.

"Stop him!" a bride yelled.

"Death to the damned!" yelled the bandleader.

He raised the dagger and charged at Leonardo. Cesar stepped in front of the bandleader, who then stabbed him just below the ribcage. The bandleader pulled him in close. The blade tented the back of Cesar's blazer as it thrust entirely through him. Caesar's body began to crumple in bits of ash. The crowd panicked, letting out screams and gasps as they dispersed in a mob. The bandleader withdrew the dagger and continued to charge at Leonardo, who sluggishly turned toward the oncoming threat. He stumbled as he attempted to take a fighting stance.

The priest raised his staff and took aim; the ruby released a bolt of red lightning. The bandleader stopped in his tracks, his limbs seizing from the blast.

"Freedom! Freedom!" he screamed.

Several vampires jumped on him as he continued to rant. They used sharp claws to tear into him. The bodies of those attempting to subdue him concealed most of the activity. Pieces of his mask flew into the air.

"Get him out of here," commanded the priest, and the imposter was hauled off before anyone could get a close look at him.

Daniel looked up when several guests rushed down the hall. He cautiously walked to the edge of the stairs, where he saw Leonardo stalking drunkenly toward Jessica, determined to claim his prize.

Jessica reacted very little to the events; her emotions had already vacated. Leonardo grabbed her by the elbow, and she offered no resistance. He then locked eyes with Daniel. For a moment, Daniel was frozen with uncontrollable fright. With a leer, Leonardo hauled Jessica down the stairs and around the corner.

Through the commotion, the priest glimpsed Leonardo hauling Jessica to another area of the house. With staff still in hand, he raised the notepad to his face to read more clearly; he glanced over to the brides huddled in a group for safety by a security detail of vampires, still wearing their official police uniforms. It was as he guessed; twenty-five brides were huddled together. Leonardo's quota had been met.

Daniel still stood in place, his heart drumming in his throat. He knew that Leonardo would not easily forget his face. He had to get out of there.

Daniel returned to the room, quickly scooped together his belongings, and followed some guests heading for the other end of the hall. He thought there might be a back exit, and fortunately for him there was. He quickly looked at their necks, just to make sure he wasn't mixed in with the wrong crowd.

"That was crazy," one exclaimed.

"I know. Let's get outta here," said another.

The group of five, tailed by Daniel, rushed down a narrow set of stairs that let out on the porch in the rear of the house. Bright lights from police mobiles seared around the sides of the house to light up the trees and lawn; their loud sirens blasted away the suburban silence. Wanting no part of a police investigation, Daniel and the group headed toward an ivy-covered fence at the foot of the backyard.

Daniel looked back to see if they were being followed, but got an eyeful of something else through a vast glass door. Before the backdrop of an immense kitchen, Leonardo wrapped his left hand around the small of Jessica's back and leaned toward her neck with fangs bared. He walked his fingertips up and down her neckline.

"Hurry up," an escaping guest said to Daniel.

He made it to the fence and was helped over by two others.

"Just keep running. Don't look back," said one to the other; Daniel took it under his own advisement.

He was good at running and always had been. Some things never change. Some things were what they were.

⇒+ +⇐

Some things were not what they seemed. Leonardo leaned in. "You didn't think I would forget our deal, did you?" he whispered in Jessica's ear.

She gulped, the veins in her neck pulsated.

"Are you sure you want to do this?"

"Yes," Jessica replied in a nervous, frazzled voice, closing her eyes tight.

Leonardo shivered with anticipation. "Open your eyes. I want you to look at me," he said, but Jessica did not oblige.

Leonardo raised his head for a moment and then came down slowly. His mouth opened wide, and the gold-capped fangs punctured Jessica's skin.

With a loud crash, Priest Aitlas leaped right through an adjoining wall. He grabbed Leonardo by the collar and flung him over the kitchen island into the china cupboard. The crashed glass and porcelain littered the room.

Jessica clutched at her gashed neck and, then reached for a small towel and pressed it over the wound. She looked up at the priest with tears filling her eyes.

"You may go, my dear. This is a Family matter," Priest Aitalas said.

She ran to the patio doors and threw them open. Jessica looked to the right and the left, trying to decide; then she took off toward the left. She noticed a gate cleverly disguised as a part of the ivy-covered wall and escaped through it and into the dark curtain of the night.

CHAPTER 5

A STRAY

It was going to be a long trip back to the other side of South Central. Daniel noticed a Magic Transport waiting booth. But as he read the schedule by the dim light of distant storefronts, he saw that the Magic Transport had stopped running several hours ago.

It would take him hours to walk home, but it was better than being caught in a roundup. He decided to walk along the path of the Magic Transport.

"Where did you go wrong, Daniel?" he asked as he trudged along. "Well, at least you tried. Otherwise, you would always wonder…"

But a horrible feeling soon descended on Daniel—a gnawing sense that he hadn't done wrong by going to the drink ceremony but that maybe he hadn't gone far enough. Instead of finding the bravery to save Jessica, he had opted to save himself.

Nights were especially dark in Anthrazit. Most merchants turned off all their lights to cut costs. But the smog had subsided, and the air felt mild and cool. Without the constant noise of people and mobiles, it was almost peaceful.

Daniel kept a brisk pace. The sidewalk of the roadway became dusty and blended with the thin pavement, leaving nothing but a thick rush of air between him and the red mobile that whizzed by. A young woman hung from the window, hollering with glee. The mobile's taillights became dots, and slowly disappeared into the night.

Daniel began to wonder what had become of the few people he considered to be friends while in grade school. He was sure that those who could had already moved to Central District and made something of themselves.

He heard another mobile coming up behind him. It was emerald green, still in mint condition, and slowed just ahead.

"Looks like you could use a ride. Hop in," said the driver with slurred speech. The three boys cramped in the cabin were barely conscious.

"No, thanks. I'm good," Daniel replied. "Actually, I'm really close now. But thanks."

The driver turned to his friends, and they shared a loud laugh. The young man stepped on the accelerator and sped off, leaving Daniel in a plume of coal smoke.

Daniel let out a series of coughs as he rested his hands on his knees. The smoke he accidentally inhaled scorched his lungs, and the pain was almost enough to bring him to the ground. His eyes became red and filled with tears.

"I had no idea it was that bad," he thought. As the vehicle made off into the distance, its smoke was lighter in color than the exhaust from an average mobile. He was certain that the green mobile was using a liquid coal engine, which could enhance the speed of the vehicle at the risk of your life. Liquid was a highly flammable substance, and extensive exposure would tear the lungs to shreds.

Daniel kept on, letting out long, careful coughs to clear the phlegm produced by the car's exhaust. Perhaps a mile later, he was bathed in light from behind. He moved over further from the road, to make sure he was in no danger of being run over. The vast vehicle rumbled by, the greenish light illuminating a series of windows. It was a Magic Transport! There were no passengers on board, and the transports had long since stopped running, but there it was. Fifty feet ahead of Daniel, it pulled over and came to a stop. The front passenger door opened.

Daniel sprinted toward the transport, his eyes still red and teary. At the door he stopped, panting, and looked up. It was the same driver who had dropped him off earlier in the day. He was busy making more notes in his ledger.

"You again?" he barked. "Hey, kid, what are you doing? Can't you see I've got a mountain load of things to do here?"

"Sorry, sir," Daniel replied, still attempting to recover from his run. "Can I have a lift? I don't have any money but—"

"Are you serious? What do you take me for? You kids today think anything is yours for the asking, don't you? Always thinking you're entitled to whatever you want," the jaded driver ranted, although, his eyes remained kind and welcoming.

"No, sir. I can pay you back," Daniel responded.

"Which way are you heading?"

"East Main Street."

"Okay, get in," said the driver, caving to this outwardly helpless young man.

"Thank you, thank you. I promise I will pay you back," Daniel said in a rush as he climbed aboard.

"Just stay toward the back," the driver responded.

Daniel got in and sat in the very last row, and the transport rumbled on. The dark landscape crawled by outside, and soon the rocking motion of the drive lulled him to sleep.

CHAPTER 6
TRAMP

Daniel awoke suddenly. Where was he? How long had he been asleep?

The night was pitch dark, and the driver was pulling up to a stop Daniel had never seen. He grabbed his bag and briskly walked toward the front.

"Do you think you can find your way from here?" asked the driver.

Daniel stood next to him and peered out the front windshield. The street signs had familiar names, but this section was foreign to him.

"This is good. Thank you so much," Daniel responded. He was uncertain but did not want to appear ungrateful for the favor. He exited the Magic Transport, placing his feet on the grimy stone pavement. "What's your name? How can I contact you to repay you?"

"Don't worry, kid. I'm sure I'll see you again," the driver replied, giving Daniel a long stare and a wink. He pulled a lever to close the door and drove off into the early-morning haze.

The streets were vacant, which suited Daniel just fine. After walking for about thirty minutes, he found himself along his regular path leading to the empty dam. He'd begun thinking about the contest again. It was now two days away. Would Jessica stay true to her word? Daniel needed to devise a new plan to raise the necessary funds.

"Maybe I can get a few more portraits done. A couple really nice ones would be worth a healthy price," he thought. He veered away from the dam, heading back toward the central area of the parish. A few hours later, he reached the hostel where he had been staying until two weeks before.

It was a red brick building, four stories tall, with a gray metal door and dark-green molding at the top. He turned the knob and pushed the door open. Unfortunately for the residents, the absentee owner had neglected to get the lock repaired. The hall was narrow, and the sage-green paint was chipped and crumbling from the walls, showing the dull white primer beneath it. Daniel approached a small broom closet housed below the stairway. When he pulled it open, three broom handles jumped out at him. He pushed them aside and picked up a beaten canvas bag with a wooden folded homemade easel attached, which doubled as a harness.

"When are you coming back for the rest of your stuff?" a gruff voice interrupted.

Daniel didn't panic. It was the janitor, a homely man with sagging skin, whose lower jaw hung when he spoke and while he was thinking. He had several missing teeth and deep indentations where his fangs used to be.

"Two weeks," Daniel replied. "I just need two more weeks." He attached the easel bag to his shoulders and held his khaki bag by his side.

"They won't hold your things forever," replied the janitor, dragging his words. Daniel nodded and turned to walk out.

"Oh, someone came by looking for you. A man in a white suit," said the janitor. The man—the one who had been yapping in Jessica's ear. The one who'd called him a wide-eyed admirer.

"What did he say?" Daniel replied eagerly. "Was it about the contest?"

He recalled that he'd briefly mentioned to Jessica that he was staying at the hostel. At the time, it sounded more palatable than admitting he was a squatter, living in an old dam.

"Wait here." The janitor opened a small room to the right and entered, slamming the door behind him. There was a small sign on the door that read "Authorized Personnel Only."

After several minutes, he emerged with a small white envelope and handed it to Daniel. The envelope bore his name and had Jessica's scent on it. He opened the envelope hastily and pulled out the rose-pink paper contained within. His heart started to race. The short note read:

> *Daniel,*
> *Sorry our time together came to such a quick end.*
> *I would love to see you again and explain everything.*
> *Please meet me at S-CAP's small south entrance at*
> *eight. See you tonight.*
> *Sincerely,*
> *Jessica*

"I'm not a mailbox, you know," said the janitor disapprovingly. Daniel nodded and shook his hand vigorously.

⋯⋯

Back in his underground lair, Daniel lay fully awake. He had hoped to nap for a few hours, but that turned out to be impossible. He scratched at the stubble on his cheek.

"Oh, no!" Daniel exclaimed as he looked at his thumb. His fingernail had somehow grown gnarled. When had that happened? He opened his hand and looked at the nails on his left hand and then his right hand. All of his nails were in some stage of overgrowth.

"Every time I get to see her, I break out with something completely gross," Daniel muttered. He scratched a nervous itch behind his ear. "I wonder what she meant by 'explain everything.'"

Daniel found a pair of scissors and attempted to cut his crusted nails, but the scissors proved to be too weak. "I can't let her see me like this," he exclaimed. Then he remembered what Jessica told him while they sat in the study: "If you want something, you'll find a way."

Daniel pulled out a roll of blue-backs. He only had five hundred left, but now that his rent was free, he was making it last. He took out a few bills and stuffed the rest under the mattress.

The midmorning commerce had picked up in the marketplace. As Daniel strode through, he spotted a familiar grooming shop, a fixture since he was a child. The windowed storefront had a dark-purple trim and a blue-and-white, broadly striped awning. In bright yellow letters, the sign read: "Sol Grooming." Daniel opened the door, and a tiny golden bell above the entry let out a jingle.

"How may I help you?" asked the shopkeeper.

She was stocky and in her sixties, wearing stripes that matched her store. She wore a pair of silver-rimmed glasses that had a black string attached at the ends of the frame. Her puffy cheeks sagged a little, and a mole sprouted up from her right cheek.

"I need to prepare for a very special evening," Daniel responded.

She stepped back and visually inspected the young man before her. She folded her arms and began to circle him.

"You need a lot of work," she commented. "Something custom tailored for sure."

"Is there something off the rack that could work?" Daniel replied.

She snickered. "Let's get you cleaned up first, and we'll take it from there."

Daniel stuck out his hands.

"Oh, dear," she yelped. Then she turned toward the back of the store. "Olga!"

Grooming shops were one of the few highlights in Anthrazit, frequented by the few very well-off citizens. A resident could fully clean up and rejuvenate from prolonged exposure to the commonwealth's elements. Special showers and chemical peels were capable of removing toxins from the skin. After that, one could sit in white leather chairs or lie on white leather beds and be groomed from head to toe. But only if one could afford it.

Daniel ordered a simple head, hands, and foot treatment. The shopkeeper and Olga, her tall, slim assistant, got to work trimming his hair.

"Not too short," Daniel interjected, and as they lifted the long hanks of hair from his ears, the women looked at each other with raised eyebrows.

They combed his hair down to conceal the pointed tips and then continued to his unsightly nails. The shopkeeper left Olga to carry on while she began to rummage through a bin of rejected clothes.

"So why didn't you go to one of the grooming parlors in Central? That's where everyone goes nowadays," said the shopkeeper.

"Sorry, I thought you could use the business. Now I know better for next time," Daniel replied.

"Oh, he's feisty. I like him," responded Olga.

"You'll be surprised how much a man's confidence grows after getting cleaned up a little," the shopkeeper replied. "You do look much better. Stand up, smarty pants." She held back a proud smile. "Stop slouching."

Daniel stood with his arms by his side, dressed in the white robe of the grooming shop. The cut ends of his hair littered the shoulders of the robe.

The shopkeeper tossed a few garments at him. "Go into that fitting room and try these on," she instructed.

Daniel strutted out in an ill-fitting outfit.

"Nope."

Daniel retreated and returned.

"Absolutely not."

Daniel went through several rounds, finally stepping out in a pair of dark-gray slim jeans, a white dress shirt open at the collar, a red button-down sweater that was rolled to just below his elbows, and a diagonally striped tie hanging loosely around his neck. But he still wore the same old boots and beanie hat that he always had.

"Red seems to be your color," she said. "But why do you cling to those old things? Sometimes you have to let go if you want to make a real change."

Daniel responded to the advice by hanging his head.

"She is a lucky girl, whoever she is," the shopkeeper continued.

Daniel partially looked up, his cheeks almost as red as the sweater.

⊯ ⊯

It was seven-thirty when Daniel arrived early at the rendezvous. As visitors piled out of the main south exit, Daniel sat and looked on from the ledge of a four-foot-tall concrete wall. He could hear the mixture of animated chatter of children giving accounts of their experiences, reporting in extensive detail as though the parent or guardian had not been there with them the entire time.

Eight o'clock came and went, and Daniel still sat wearing his new threads, still holding a healthy bunch of yellow lilies. They were expensive and freshly cut from the hydroponic florist near the groomer, the one sure to have been the source of Jessica's trace scent. His hands were getting sweaty again. He cupped his hand before his mouth and blew to confirm that his breath was not offensive.

After almost an hour, Daniel's heart began to give up. Had she changed her mind? He wished he had a talkie. At least then he'd be able to call Ms. Winters at the office and check to see if they were still on.

With no security station in sight, Daniel got to his feet and walked toward the service door, which was tucked away, just out of plain view. He turned the handle, and it clacked loudly as it turned the catch. "Is this how it usually goes?" he thought. "A woman may leave the door open, but I've got to be man enough to walk through it?" Being an only child raised by an unmarried priest had not provided many lessons in how to engage the opposite sex.

The service exit was part of a larger door made for docking oversized mobiles. Daniel made his way down the wide docking hall. He held the lilies close to his chest for safekeeping as he moved through the poorly lit hall. The path ahead grew more ominous; a few sickly and agitated animals sat in cages on either side. They howled and barked at Daniel from behind the bars of their cages. Daniel realized that he might have made a grave error—it didn't seem likely that Jessica had meant for him to enter in this manner. And there was no security. He turned around. The light from the street poured through the open door.

He would wait back on the street—in here, he might miss her. As he walked toward the door, he was seized suddenly from behind. The flowers fell to the ground as a rough sack was thrust over his head. Daniel pushed and twisted, trying to escape, but there were too many strong arms holding him back. Then his head was knocked back, and pain exploded through his jaw.

CHAPTER 7

RITE OF PASSAGE

Daniel Griffin's eyes opened slowly. His lip tasted like a bloody, raw piece of meat, which was a terrible experience for him as a strict vegetarian who was squeamish at the very sight of blood, much less his own. As the warm, rich-crimson blood flowed out from his swollen lips and other cuts and bruises all over his face, the realization seeped in. Daniel was hit so hard that he had completely blacked out.

"He's awake," scoffed a voice.

Daniel's eyes were crusted over with a mixture of dirt and tears. All he could distinguish were three blurry silhouettes. One of them walked closer and bent down to look at Daniel, who was still doubled over on the rough cobblestone pavement. The figure's eyes glowed like red neon signs.

"Come on. Get up," he whispered in Daniel's ear.

The figure stood up and stepped back. Daniel squinted and rubbed his eyes, which confirmed what he already knew. It was Leonardo.

Leonardo towered over Daniel. He wore a long, dark leather jacket with several straps held by large gold-plated buckles. His hair was still slicked back, and his pale skin was almost bluish white; he was more at ease than he was at the drink ceremony.

"Couldn't wait to get out of that stifling suit. This is more my style," Leonardo said. "Don't worry. I'm not going to bite you." He offered a deceiving smirk.

Daniel wondered whether this was the end of a lesson not to cross the young governor, or if he was just being set up to be turned after all. Leonardo licked his gold-capped fangs.

"Honestly, you are too weak for my taste," he continued.

Leonardo's two oversized companions rushed in and grabbed Daniel, forcing him to stand, and held him up between them. Daniel threw his lightweight frame into their hands, relying on the henchmen for support.

"I like something with more of a backbone, more fight to it," Leonardo said, continuing his monologue.

Daniel's mind started to drift as he wondered how this would end. Leonardo could tell he didn't have his full attention. He charged over and socked Daniel in the ribs.

"And a bit more respect!" he yelled.

Daniel screamed and caved to the pain. The two henchmen wouldn't let him fall to the ground, though, almost as if to say, "You are stronger than that." But Daniel knew better. Henchmen like those didn't think. The healed double puncture wounds and the whitened pupils were all the evidence he needed that these two drones had lost any will to think independently a long time ago.

"Forget it. I'm wasting my breath. Just toss him in," Leonardo said flippantly.

With vacant stares, the henchmen headed toward the railing of the lioness pit. Daniel experienced a sudden rush of adrenalin, brought on by a revelation. If he didn't fight back somehow, this really would be the end. He placed the heel of his ragged boot on the railing and pushed back with all the strength left in his weak frame.

"No, wait! Stop," he squealed. "There is nothing going on between me and Jessica. I swear it."

Leonardo had already started walking away, but he stopped and looked over his shoulder. Daniel got his opening.

"I know you really like her. I can see it. I'm sure she sees it too. She hasn't consented yet?" Daniel attempted to charm the dangerously volatile Leonardo on a bluff. "Is that what this is all about?"

Leonardo turned around, took a step toward Daniel, and shrugged. The two henchmen, like automatons, had no reaction.

"Governor, I'm nobody. I could never give her the things you could. She will come around; she just needs a little time, you know. Women, right?" Daniel tried to chuckle, but it was more of a pain-filled cough.

Leonardo placed his hands in his pockets and hung his head. He pulled out a pack of cigarettes, carefully plucking one. He pulled an embroidered gold-plated lighter from the other pocket. He lit the cigarette, took a long draw, and held his head up, blowing a big puff into the air. It was dark, but he could still see the thick smog that covered the commonwealth like a cocoon.

"I...I know how you can win her over. I can really help you out, man. I know the things she likes." Daniel talked deliriously, offering himself up for a life of servitude.

Most vampires would not pass up an open invitation to have a new-bitten lackey, especially not Leonardo. But it seemed there was a first time for everything.

"Daniel, I'm sorry, but I have no real use for you," Leonardo responded with a sinisterly polite rejection and walked away briskly.

"No! Governor Leonardo," Daniel shouted, but it was too little, too late.

The henchmen grabbed him and tossed him in like a ragdoll. Daniel landed in the pit. He heard a growl inside the cave and scurried to his feet. Then she emerged. Teresa was larger than she appeared from the height of the den's cliff, and Daniel lost his breath just at the sight of her. Teresa was still clear across the pit, but she had locked eyes with him and was laser focused.

In a last-ditch effort, Daniel broke his gaze and made for the steep edges of the pit. In a futile exercise, he grasped at loose soil and twigs. He could not grip the smooth rock surface. Teresa was now heading toward him, and there was nowhere to run.

Whack! His head hit the rocks as Teresa smacked him against them with her right front paw. She had reached him quickly. Now with his back to the ground, she stood over him. Unlike Leonardo, Teresa was hungry and not in the mood to play with a much-needed meal.

He tried to shuffle up onto his elbows. Teresa pounced on him, and he collapsed to his back again. She began to use her front paws to stretch him out and shred his sweater and shirt, looking for something worth taking a bite of. The trauma of his present circumstance brought on a childhood memory in vivid detail.

Maybe it was the eyes, or the ears, or just being physically incapable of standing up for himself, but Daniel always seemed to be the subject of loathing while growing up.

He was the sole orphan who lived at the South Central Parish. The usually emotionally distant Father

Frank was the only support he had ever known. It was very common that Daniel would return home to the parish at the end of the school day, covered with bruises. Father Frank would draw a warm basin of water and dissolved salts and arm himself with a towel over the shoulder to take care of Daniel's welts and cuts. One day, Daniel returned home wanting more than just the ritualistic cleaning; he sought answers.

"Why?" sniffled Daniel, his nose looking like a bloody punching bag.

When Father Frank took off his shirt, Daniel's body was filled with clusters of bruises. Father Frank gritted his teeth.

"I ran as hard as I could. I hid when I could. And I prayed they wouldn't catch me. Why did they catch me, Father?" Daniel pleaded.

Father Frank was an austere man, and no one would confuse his portly figure for the making of a jolly personality. His grim face came by the daily exercise of pushing away all emotion. With barely a hint of empathy, he took Daniel firmly by the wrists.

"Daniel, sometimes you will pray with all your heart for God to shut the mouths of the lions, and he doesn't. Do you know why?" Father Frank inquired in an instructional manner.

Daniel's eyes shifted to the upper left as he dug deep into his thoughts for an answer.

"No," he replied.

Father Frank leaned forward and replied delicately, "Because maybe, just maybe, he wants you to open yours."

⇥ ⇤

The memory of that small interaction with Father Frank became lucid to the point that Daniel was emotionally transported to that moment in time, and he relived it afresh. He did consider it crazy, and desperate, but that memory triggered a strong urge in him. He grabbed Teresa by the shoulder, and as she bit him, Daniel bit right back.

He could feel her warm blood and life drain into him. At first the sensation was repulsive, but as her blood filled his mouth, he couldn't help feeling pleasure. He swallowed, and then the awareness of what he was doing struck him, and he released her. Teresa the lioness was just as shocked, and backed up just for a moment. As Daniel remained confused about the compulsion that overtook him, something truly unexpected began to happen. Daniel's body began to transform.

Muscles appeared where there were none, and more muscles appeared on top of those. It felt like something was tearing him apart from the inside out. His eyes burned like fire. Every nerve ending in his body writhed in pain that made everything before faint in comparison. He grew in mass and size. Fur sprouted from his skin. Soon, Teresa became the one experiencing fear.

Daniel moved toward her. As he tried to speak, all that came out was a low, rumbling growl. Teresa sprang a quick 180-degree turn and retreated to her cave. Daniel's hearing was now razor-sharp, and he could hear guards approaching from a far distance. He leaped on the embankment, and his long, sharp claws gouged along the rocks as he swiftly made his way out of the pit. The beast that was once Daniel disappeared into rugged brushes at the edge of the lioness's habitat.

⊷⊹⊹⊶

About an hour later, on the eastern side of South Central, Father Frank had all but turned in for the night. The lamps were out in the main sanctuary, but he sat in the back pew reading the *Metro Daily* paper. Daniel had often gotten on his case for this habit.

"You will ruin your eyesight," Daniel used to nag.

But he no longer lived with Father Frank. He had moved out almost a year before. His sudden departure came on the heels of a heated argument. Daniel had felt a need to see the world for himself and was also frustrated by living under someone else's authority. Father Frank had a different view of the events, but the result was all the same.

Father Frank paused for a moment. The memory of how Daniel and he separated still haunted him. He held his head up to look at the mural on the ceiling. It was Daniel's interpretation of the Garden of Eden. It was crude in some areas, but showed passion and real talent. It was the first project he had ever seen Daniel take such ownership over, working on it every day after school and weekends, without any prodding. After Daniel's grave illness, it was just the thing to bring them together. Those were the happiest memories Father Frank shared with him.

There was an urgent knock at the door. He stood, and walked toward the entrance, somewhat unwillingly. He slid the large deadbolts on the door, and pulled on the wrought-iron handle to open one of the immense wooden double doors. He began with his eyes partly closed and exhausted from a long day.

"The parish is closed for the..." He hesitated when he noticed the uniformed officer.

"Father, please keep the doors closed. We have imposed an emergency curfew," the officer announced.

Gazing past the officer, he could see several people making haste to get home or indoors, while a number of officers hurried the stragglers along.

"What's the commotion?" Father Frank asked, not making eye contact with the officer.

"One of the wild animals has escaped from the zoo," he replied.

"Wild animal?"

He turned to look at the officer, but the man's puncture marks caught his attention first. Being bitten is your chance at upward mobility in Anthrazit, just as the brochures stated, but it was only if the vampire clan decided you were fit for skilled labor; they could decide that you weren't good enough, in which case you became the main course—a fate Father Frank always feared for Daniel.

"Everyone must remain inside until daylight," said the officer, asserting some of that middle-management bravado. His fangs, like those of most bitten skilled workers, were underwhelming.

"See you in the morning...or not," replied Father Frank.

Most skilled workers had the advantage of being day walkers, something most would gladly trade for a bit more power, authority, and prestige. The stronger the vampire gene was in a turned individual, the more sensitive they were to light and extreme temperatures of hot and cold.

Father Frank bolted the door again and began walking down the aisle of the parish. Suddenly there was a huge crash on the roof and loud scratching noises in the roof stairwell. His heart leapt into his throat. That stairway led into a large but cluttered back room that Daniel had called home for many years.

The door creaked open, and a dark, tall, monstrous figure emerged. At eight feet tall, it stood on its hind legs like a man. The creature had long hair like a lion's mane, an irregular snout, and glowing yellow eyes. It slowly made its way toward Father Frank. He was completely terrified and instantly froze in place.

"Father."

The word could barely be understood beneath the heavy, breathy growl. But the tone of the gentle voice beneath it all was still recognizable to the guardian that raised him.

"Daniel?" Father Frank replied.

The creature collapsed to the marble floor and shape-shifted back into the form of a young man. Father Frank took off the short blanket he had over his shoulders and covered Daniel's bruised body.

CHAPTER 8
COUNTERPARTS

It was morning, and Daniel was asleep on the same old cot in the same cramped room he grew up in as a boy. He tossed and turned, fully immersed in a vivid and familiar dream. Daniel had experienced this sleep-induced vision several times while growing up.

In the dream, Daniel imagined himself moving rapidly through a forest. The air was thick with fog, similar to Anthrazit, yet different. The air around him moved quickly and felt wet, like droplets of water suspended in midair. It was free of the cleaning-fluid smell that was a signature of the commonwealth. The trees were different too. Though Daniel had a paradigm for what a forest might be like, and though there were trees in Anthrazit, they were not as numerous as what he had seen in his schoolbooks; the trees in his dream had no leaves and had dangerously sharp branches. The sky was dark but not concealed in smog. Strange dragon-like creatures flew through the sky just above the tree line; they were his references for the fantasy creature drawings in his sketchbooks. It was difficult to tell if they were pursuing him. Except for the shapes of the flying creatures and strange trees zipping by, many of the details in his dream were covered in mysterious shadow and haze, much like an incomplete drawing.

He heard a grunt and looked down to find he was riding a leathery creature, running as fast as it could with Daniel on its back. It had wings but kept them tucked by its side. "Don't worry, Daniel, I'll keep you safe. I promise." These words from the creature were enough to jolt him out of the dream.

Daniel flailed his arms wildly. He tumbled out of the undersized bed, hitting the floor, and awoke startled. Daniel made his way back to the bed, wondering if everything, including the night before, was just a dream. He touched his side. It was still tender, and he raised his shirt to examine the wound. The occurrence of the night before was inescapable, and no amount of sleep was about to undo that reality. The wounds were still pink at the edges, the punctures puffy and likely infected. Nevertheless, he was healing much faster than was humanly possible.

Anxiety began to fill his mind. "What am I?" he wondered. "Could I have been a vampire all this time and not known it?" His hands began to shake. Even as he attempted to reason through the experience, Daniel attempted to repress the feeling of pleasure, power, and strength he felt in the first moments after biting Teresa.

It was a very strange series of events that somehow brought him back to the parish, but he was not surprised that he ended up there. This was certainly not the set of circumstances under which he wanted to return to Father Frank. He wished it were a triumphal entry with a pronouncement of "Look what I've done with my life." Invading the sanctuary as some sort of beast was a far cry from that hope.

Almost a year before, they had been arguing, and both were in too deep before they realized how their tempers had flared. Father Frank grabbed Daniel by the collar, and his hand got caught in the links of the chain attached to Daniel's pendant, the one treasured item he had in his possession on the day he found him as a toddler. As he tugged, the chain snapped, and the pendant fell to the ground, the links scattering in every direction. Daniel became angry, snarling and yelling right back at Father Frank. He had never seen such fire in Daniel. As the argument escalated, neither would back down.

"You are a liar, a hypocrite, and a fake!" shouted Daniel.

It was that precise moment when their relationship was severed. Irreparably cut by words Daniel wished immediately after that he could unspeak.

Father Frank staggered back, almost as if he was stabbed through the heart. He nodded, not uttering a word. He turned his back to Daniel and knelt at the altar, praying quietly. Daniel knelt next him, issuing words of apology. He was truly contrite, kneeling next to his guardian for over an hour, Father praying quietly, and Daniel praying audibly that God would help Father Frank to forgive him. The damage was irreversible; Daniel stood and went to his room. He packed as many items as he could and left the sanctuary, the only home he had ever known.

Now there he was, back in the same place, almost an unwanted guest in the room of his childhood memories. It was still very early in the morning, but Daniel thought he should do a few things around the parish to make himself useful, providing a peace offering of sorts and earning newfound favor with the old man. A faint morning light barely made it through the dirt-encrusted stained-glass windows, but it kept trying. At the front of the church, above the large doors, was the centerpiece: a circular stained-glass mosaic of the Last Supper, with many of the apostle figures faded and obscured by layers of grime on the outer and inner sides of the glass.

Father Frank hobbled down the narrow spiral staircase that connected his living annex to the church. The sanctuary had three columns of pews separated by narrow aisles. The wooden floor was dusty, worn, and in bad need of a new varnish. In the back of the church stood a one-piece stone pedestal embedded in the floor. It came to a modest holy-water stoup.

Father Frank saw Daniel across the row of pews, sweeping, and straightening books in the holders of the backs of the pews. He was heartily making short work of having things look presentable, a chore he had performed routinely in his adolescence.

"No need. It's rush hour, and they ain't rushin' here," said Father Frank, dismissing any importance of what Daniel was doing. "Besides, you aren't an altar boy or anything of the sort anymore."

He continued with a waddle-like limp toward the front of the church, his back now to Daniel.

"What happened since I left? You were like that tough old bird at S-CAP. Set in your ways and having things a certain way," Daniel teased.

"That bird is dead now," Father Frank snapped.

Daniel was speechless, hardly able to reason how that had slipped his memory. Father Frank got to the front and began to drag an old leather trunk that was too heavy to lift.

"Let me get that," Daniel responded almost apologetically.

He quickly made his way over but had just as much trouble lifting the trunk and resorted to pushing it down the aisle, finally parking it against the back wall. Daniel walked toward Father Frank, a bit winded, but he stood hoping for a little note of praise and a break in the tension. The stout old man pointed at the pew next to them.

"Sit down!" Father Frank yelled.

Daniel took a seat at the end of the pew. Father Frank clutched the edge of the pew in front and pushed against it. Daniel thought if he had the strength, he would have ripped it right out of the floor.

"Truth be told, I'm not a merciful man. But when I found you that night as a little boy. Stuffed..." He choked up and stopped to clear his throat, his eyes turning red as he tried to restrain his tears. "A lot of women have come to those doors, hoping to leave their latest indiscretion. I would cut them off in the middle of their predictable sad story and send them off to Grace General."

The old man took another breath. Daniel knew enough not to interrupt.

"But on that fateful night fifteen years ago—I can't even remember why I was in that stairwell—I heard you crying because somebody had stuffed you, a two-year-old, into the hands of that statue on the roof. I thought to myself, Who does that?"

"Father Frank—" Daniel finally decided to verbally engage his custodian.

"I raised you like my own flesh and blood," Father Frank kept going, stomping on any words Daniel offered. "I just asked one thing of you: do not give in to those half-dead bastards because the moment you do, they will own you."

"Father Frank, they didn't turn me."

"Show me! Show me where they bit you," Father Frank railed as he grabbed at Daniel's shirt, the boy pushing his hands away.

"They didn't bite me," Daniel replied.

"I saw it!"

The father's yelling was at fever pitch. He pulled at Daniel's shirt to confirm the evidence of what he saw the night before.

"It's a bite but not from them."

Daniel raised his shirt to reveal large, deep wounds, but they had healed over almost as if they had occurred several years prior. Father Frank stumbled back. Daniel looked to the floor, ashamed.

"Oh my God," Father Frank gasped.

"I have not joined the vampires. I was bitten by the lioness at the preserve. I don't know how I made it back here and how I healed so quickly. I'm not really sure what I am," Daniel confessed.

Father Frank wasn't buying a word of Daniel's story so far, but the shock and disappointment on his face were already too much, and so Daniel left out the detail of biting Teresa.

"I had a really bad run-in with the new governor. Someone invited me to a party where he was going to be. I wasn't going to go, but there was this woman that I really liked. I really wanted to meet her. Actually I thought I could talk her out of pledging. Not only did I not talk her out of it, but Leonardo caught up with me and beat the crap out of me. Then he threw me in the lion's pit," Daniel explained. "Honestly, I would have joined if it meant saving my life," he admitted. "But he rejected me, tossing me in and saying I wasn't even worth the effort."

"You didn't take all your belongings when you left. I'll get them," Father Frank replied coldly.

"You are throwing me out?" Daniel responded with a stunned look.

"You're the one who left. This isn't your home anymore."

Daniel sat and folded his hands, resting them on the pew in front, and tucked his head under them. He wanted to cry, but he pushed the emotion away as he had learned from Father Frank. With a few more sniffles, the anguish was gone, and he began to fix his shirt.

Just then, Daniel caught the scent of something beautiful and familiar. He looked up, and there she was, Ms. Jessica Winters.

She was sharply dressed in a long black coat, with a thin, translucent shawl around her neck. Her shiny black hair was slicked back and held perfectly in place by the same gold embroidered stone barrette with a wood--like texture. She wore large, dark sunglasses, accessorizing an impenetrable, almost perfect exterior. "Has she been turned?" Daniel wondered.

From his first encounter with Jessica, he saw a glimpse of a heart that was wild and passionate, yet playful. "An encounter with a heart like that I would not survive," he thought. "Either way..."

"Daniel," said Jessica.

She was now standing right in front of him. He was so entranced by her, that he didn't even notice when she had gracefully made her way through the pews from across the sanctuary.

"Ms. Winters...I mean, Dr. Winters—" He bashfully made his way to his feet. "What are you doing here?"

She smiled but gave no verbal response. She removed her shades to reveal dark, piercing eyes.

"Sorry, I guess that was kind of a personal question. Or not. After all, it is a church, where people pray and..." Daniel paused his rambling only due to a shortage of words.

"Are you free for coffee?" Her voice was mild, yet assertive.

Daniel held his head down, looking up occasionally as Jessica awaited his response.

Father Frank entered in just enough time to see Daniel following behind Jessica, but he couldn't tell who she was. The heavy doors closed behind them with a loud thud.

⋯⋯

It was now midmorning. The sky was hazy, and there was a sense that the only sunlight that the oversized town got was reflected leftovers that barely made it through layers and layers of fog. The cobblestone streets were bustling with many pedestrians, and a few mobiles made their way through the crowds.

Several blocks from the parish was one of South Central's bright spots, an upscale coffee shop by the name of Café Milo. This establishment sat at the corner of the busiest intersection of the district and was one of the few shops that had street-side seating. Café Milo ran loud, gigantic air purifiers to make their outdoor seating more comfortable. It was pricey, and the beverages were merely decent, but if you asked any well-to-do person who frequented the shop, the typical response was, "Well, obviously no one goes there for the coffee."

Jessica and Daniel shared a small table barely big enough for one person. He continued to avoid making eye contact with her. As the wait staff ran from one table to another, the two were left alone for some time, but had not exchanged any words. Jessica swapped her shades for steel rectangle-framed glasses that somehow made her eyes even more magnetic.

"How old were you when you made the murals at the church?" she asked, attempting to break the ice.

"Ten…twelve, I forget."

"You have a real gift."

Daniel kept looking over his shoulder into the crowd of hasty pedestrians and offering no response. Jessica leaned closer, resting her elbows on the table. She reached across the small surface, thinking to take his hand, but hesitated. "Daniel, is something the matter?"

Daniel pivoted quickly; they were now nose to nose.

"Your eyes? Are they two different—" Jessica started, but Daniel pulled away before she could finish. "That is remarkable! Let me see. I won't stare...well, kind of. Please?" Her playful demeanor caused him to relax a little.

"People usually look away. The two different colors can be like looking at two different people and never quite a whole person," Daniel admitted.

"I don't mind."

She leaned forward, and her shawl dropped gently to reveal an unsightly two-track scar across her neck. Jessica pulled back swiftly and used both hands to fix the shawl around her neck. She looked down, her eyes shifting from side to side in search of the appropriate words.

"The mural project contest is postponed until the investigation is cleared regarding the incident last night. Chances for getting that initiative off the ground again aren't looking good."

"I understand," Daniel replied in a disappointed voice.

"All that effort, marketing, and publicity, could all go to waste," she continued. "Honestly, I don't even care about that. They are trying to shut down the Teresa exhibit, and terminate her. I don't know what I would do if that happens." She paused to acknowledge that Daniel was still taking in the blow from the lost opportunity. "Daniel, I'm so sorry." Jessica's voice was consoling, but it brought him no immediate comfort.

"Well, that should teach me for dreaming so big," Daniel responded in a jaded tone.

"Daniel, please don't be like that," she replied. Daniel slouched back in the narrow café chair. "What are you going to do?"

"I don't know, but I'll figure something out. I have to."

"You can do anything you put your mind to. I mean that." She closed her eyes and raised her head. "First you have to make your mind up. Decide what you really want, and picture it in your imagination. Next you say it out loud. Then you go about doing what it takes to accomplish it," she concluded firmly.

As Daniel looked on, he burst into a loud, joyful laugh.

"What?" she asked inquisitively.

"That was cute, not in a childish way, but wonderful," he marveled.

"I'm glad I could amuse you," she responded with an accidentally flirtatious smile. "But I've got some serious matters to attend to, young man."

"You might act and dress older, but we are not that far apart," replied Daniel. "Miss Winters," he added sarcastically.

"Thank you, Daniel. I could really use a friend right now," she said.

Daniel's heart sunk.

"The news bureau is planning a broadcast on the speakers. The release headline reads 'Wild and Dangerous.' No one will attend her exhibit after that, I'm sure."

"What if they are right?" Daniel replied.

"The chance to study Teresa is a once-in-a-lifetime opportunity. Just imagine what we could learn from her. Most of the animals we have in the commonwealth are sick and dying, yet somehow she is unaffected, and not even a meager diet affects her health in any noticeable fashion. Teresa is temperamental but not like they have made things out to be. Something out of the ordinary happened last night. And I intend to find out what that was."

Jessica paused for a moment and placed her sleek handbag on the table in front of her.

"I should get this," Daniel interrupted, hoping to show a bit of chivalry. Without properly thinking it through, he placed his hand on hers. His heart pounded, and sounded so loud, it was hard to hear anything else.

"Don't be silly," Jessica replied, almost dismissively.

"Does she think I thought this was a date? Maybe I should not have phrased it that way. Or, worse, what if she thinks I could never afford to treat her to a simple cup of coffee?" Daniel's thoughts began to race, and he pulled his hand back suddenly.

"Thanks. I should go," said Daniel as he stood up from his chair.

"Daniel, wait...I didn't mean it like that," Jessica replied.

"I should let you get back to work. I've already taken up too much of your time," he replied politely.

He wrapped his scarf over his mouth, placed his bag over his shoulder, and stuck his hands into his pockets as he headed into the crowd of pedestrians.

———

The rest of the day was tame by comparison. Daniel spent the afternoon at his semiregular spot, a row of benches in the park just outside the animal preserve. This made an ideal locale for a starving artist. He sat with his makeshift easel in front, and the blank canvas stared back at him. He had hoped that the inclemently nice weather would bring more mothers with young kids, which were the regulars for his portrait services. But on this day, there were not so many. Commoners were miserly folk, and tighter economic times made them additionally stingy.

Daniel decided to wear the hood of his sweater over his head that day, to be less conspicuous in case someone was keeping an eye out for him. It probably didn't help much to attract parents with young children. Suddenly, a little boy ran up to him, almost knocking over the easel. He wore a toy lion's mane headpiece and carried a blue balloon tied to the back of his jacket.

"Roar!" he said playfully in an adorable, high-pitched voice.

"Timmy!" his mother yelled. "Get back here."

"Wow, little guy," Daniel responded.

"I'm the king of the jungle," Timmy declared.

"Well, your majesty, I think you are missing something very important."

Daniel took a little paint on a thin brush and painted whiskers on Timmy's round, puffy cheeks. The little boy closed his eyes with his head raised slightly to receive the adornment of silky-smooth orange and red lines of pigment. Timmy's mother approached reluctantly.

"Great. I guess you expect me to pay for that," she stated disappointedly.

She took out a few coins and tossed them in a small bowl that Daniel kept for the sake of washing his brushes. She took Timmy by the hand and led him away. Timmy looked back and made a clawing hand gesture, and Daniel raised his hand, repeating the playful gesture in return.

Daniel fished the coins from the water bowl and counted them in the palm of his glove with cutout fingers. He put them in his pocket and exhaled heavily. More than ready to call it a day, he folded up his easel and attached it to his knapsack. The easel also doubled as a harness to strengthen the knapsack. He packed in all his supplies and hoisted the bulky contraption onto his back.

He jumped over the back of the benches and made his way down the slope behind him. The bare trees at the edge of the park gave way to underdeveloped roads that led to the edges of South Central.

At the end of the dirt road stood a lone, dilapidated store next to a block of hollowed-out buildings. Daniel entered, and the buzzer went off to alert the storekeeper, though the buzzer sounded more like a wheeze. The storekeeper stuck his head out from behind the counter. He was a dark-skinned, middle-aged man wearing a star-covered beanie. After sizing up his new customer, he returned to his reading.

Just in front of the shopkeeper's counter were rows of fresh fruits, including golden-yellow apples, bright-red strawberries, and juicy, freshly sliced watermelons. Fresh goods were rare and very expensive, particularly in South Central. It was awfully tempting to just grab a couple without giving it a second thought. The owner was separated from his produce by the counter, and surely stood no chance of catching Daniel if he decided to snatch a few goods and make a dash out the door.

"Have enough respect for yourself that you will not beg or resort to stealing," said the voice of Father Frank in Daniel's head. His father figure seemed to be a part of him, ever present and challenging his conflicted desires. Daniel grabbed a no-frill can of preserved beans from the front aisle. Reaching over the tempting produce, he paid with the still-moist, paint-smeared coins.

"Thanks," said Daniel, but the shopkeeper just snatched the coins and murmured to himself as he moved further back behind his narrow counter to resume his reading, as if Daniel's patronage was a rude interruption to his day.

Daniel left the store and continued walking. There were few milestones, but he knew his way pretty well.

Splash! Daniel came to a narrow ravine and jumped in. The shallow waters streamed out of a sewer that was three feet in diameter. He entered and continued a little way to where there was a four-foot drop-off, and the ceiling opened to a cavernous space, large enough to require standing to reach up to touch the top surface. Daniel was now in his second-most frequented tunnel space, and the location of his current mural project.

Hazy daylight still shone on the ceiling and illuminated the mural: Daniel's mural, a piece still in the works, but an elaborate display of his considerable talent. It was filled with vivid colors and various animal forms practically leaping off the surface. At the center of the composition was a portrait of Jessica Winters.

He looked up and ran his fingers along various areas of his art and then took off his knapsack and sat down. He pulled out the can of beans, and opened it via the twist key built into the lid. Daniel then fetched the spoon from his bag and began to eat his supper.

"Daniel, what are you doing, man?" He spoke to himself aloud. "She totally wants you."

He then put the can away, pulled out his supplies, and got to work on his mural. When it got dark, he lit a melted wax candle held in a large glass jar and continued to work by its light. After a while, the wax was almost gone, and the jar could not hold the flame. Daniel dozed off seated and leaning against a back wall.

He fell back into the same dream he was having that morning. Sometimes the wording of what the creature said was different, or there was a variation on minor details of the scene, but it was still the same event. The dream—a muse for his fantasy drawings—was now happening with more frequency.

Daniel finally awoke and with heavy, puffy eyes decided that he was done for the evening. He started packing away his things when there was a sound from one of the distant sewer tubes. It sounded like footsteps through puddles. Then there was a low growl. Suddenly, two bright-orange eyes appeared. They blazed like they were filled with fire. The creature leaped out. It was Teresa, and she landed right in front of Daniel.

He was startled and stumbled back, but instead of attacking, the lioness backed up a little and crouched down, almost as if she was bowing to Daniel.

Daniel was stunned. This was unlike anything that had ever happened to him before.

CHAPTER 9
STUCK

Jessica Winters achieved career success a lot sooner than most. Granted, she came from a family of means, but her path up the ladder wasn't as easy as some would assume at first glance.

She stood on the balcony of her high-rise apartment, wearing black fitted jeans and a white turtleneck that covered her nose and mouth. The nights in Anthrazit were dark and quiet, but South Central District had the misfortune of also hearing the loud screeching that came from the infrequently timed railed mobiles.

Railed Mobile Transit (RMT) was an elevated set of tracks for running the mass transit within the limits of South Central District. They were crudely refurbished over-mobiles stuck together. Most still opted to walk in South Central, since the crime rate was highest at the

RMT stations, where massive cement columns seemed to crumble a bit more with every transit's passing.

But Jessica's three-bedroom condo was a paradise. The rooms were spacious and minimally decorated. The floors were polished grey marble, with flecks of silver that sparkled like diamonds. Most high-rise dwellers would not pass through their glass entryways to their balconies. But Jessica liked being on her balcony and gazing on the night skyline, covered mostly in darkness.

"Ms. Winters, this is the front desk," a crackling voice came through the intercom.

She walked over and pressed the yellow "respond" button.

"Yes?" she replied.

"The room service counter is closing up. Just wanted to make sure you didn't need anything else for the night."

"No, thank you. I'm okay."

"Very well, goodnight, ma'am," the voice replied.

With a sigh, Jessica went inside, sealing the glass doors behind her. She took off the turtleneck, revealing a workout top, a scar on her neck, and a bandage on her right forearm. Jessica stepped onto her runner's platform, a machine resembling a treadmill. It didn't use electrical power to aid in exercise, just the runner's own activity, making it harder on the user's body.

Years before, she would never have imagined this kind of a life. Her parents were accomplished doctors, and among the few who enjoyed extreme travel. They would take young Jessica in their old, beat-up mobile and drive beyond the far edges of the Anthrazit commonwealth. By the time Jessica was eleven, the family had already spent a number of trips camping in the wilderness, going as far as a day's travel. The climate was hot with fierce windstorms during the day. Night had fewer storms, but whatever animals could stand to make it a habitat came out to do their hunting. The couple would leave the mobile running, since the loud rattling kept most creatures away.

"I think we are past the worst, honey," her mom had said, and comforted a young Jessica by wrapping her arms around her as they sat nestled inside the badly shaped tent assembled by Mr. Winters.

"I'm okay," she replied.

"The tent is secure," said Mr. Winters as he barged in. "The mobile will need a good bit of coaxing to get going in the morning. That sand dust gets into everything. But it shouldn't be too much of a problem." He was an animated fellow. "Isn't this exciting?" he said eagerly.

Jessica nodded vigorously.

"Maybe we'll spot one of those wild creatures you've been wanting to see," said Mrs. Winters.

"Yeah. A really big one!" Jessica chimed in gleefully.

Tales of abnormally large animals spotted in the wilderness had been a part of Anthrazit lore for some time. Jessica loved visiting the animal preserve, but enjoyed reading children's fictional stories about creatures living in the wilderness most of all.

Her mom often joked with peers about how much Jessica loved animals. Mrs. Winters's punch line was "Jessica will be a zoologist as long as there is still one animal left in all the districts, and even after that."

There weren't many animals in Anthrazit. Domesticated animals and pets was a foreign concept. The South Central Animal Preserve's population had also been dwindling, and the remaining ones were getting sicker every year. Meat-food products were engineered from a small population of animals held in the food plants in the Industrial District. Speculative reporters were also questioning rumors as to whether these, too, were showing signs of disease.

"My fearless little snowflake. Nothing scares you, that's for sure," her dad replied. "Hey, guess what? I have a present for you." He placed his hands in his pocket and sneaked playfully toward his wife and daughter.

"Oh...huh." He stopped in his tracks and fumbled around in his pockets. "Where did it go?"

"Daddy," Jessica chided.

"Yup, there it is." He pulled out the mysterious gift and held it cuffed in his hands behind his back. "Close your eyes."

Jessica squeezed her eyes shut tight, and, without any prompting, held out her hands expectantly. Mr. Winters sat down and placed the gift in her hands.

"Now open your eyes."

Jessica looked down to see a curved petrified wooden object. It was severely crusted over with layers of hardened dirt.

"Kind of an interesting rock," Jessica remarked.

"Not just any rock—a petrified branch." He chuckled. "See how it's curved, and has holes on each side? Someone made this."

"A barrette?" Jessica responded.

"That's right. And look." Mr. Winters continued with the lesson. One area was cleaned away to reveal stunning inlaid gold ornamental details. "Whoever made it also decorated it with traces of gold."

"Oh my God. That's beautiful! Where did you find it?" Mrs. Winters was now more amazed than Jessica, realizing that her husband might have found a rare treasure. Very few ventured into the wilderness, much less wearing expensive jewelry. The piece was also unlike anything one would find in the city limits.

"Just stumbled across it during our last stop. I thought was an odd shape for a rock indeed, so I started cleaning away all the hardened dirt to discover what was underneath. Could use a lot more work to fully restore it."

"I guess you've got a new project to do when we get back home." Mrs. Winters gave Jessica a big squeeze and a kiss on the forehead.

The family had bundled in, asleep for the night. The winds had died down, when Mrs. Winters heard a strange howling.

"Dear," she began, elbowing her husband.

"Huh?" he groaned, still half asleep.

"Did you put all the food away?"

"Sure, I..." He jumped up in dismay. "I didn't. It's going to attract wolves."

"Honey, it might be too late. I think I heard something out there."

"No way! I'm not letting those things get our breakfast." He hurriedly put on his outer trench coat and exited the tent. Jessica's eyes opened barely in time to see his departure. Only a moment expired before her life changed forever.

"No! Get back," they heard him yell just before the roof of the tent was ripped apart.

It was as if someone shredded the sheltered life she wasn't aware she had lived. Three wolves stood over her father's tattered, bloody body. The leader of the pack now stood nose to nose with Mrs. Winters, who was determined to protect her only cub.

The wolf snarled; Mrs. Winters picked up a jagged slate rock and smacked it across the snout. The beast was enraged and leaped at her.

"Snowflake, run!" Mrs. Winters turned with only enough time to scream her last words.

"Mommy!" Jessica screamed.

It was too late, and three other wolves headed for her.

Jessica began running frantically as the winds picked up and worked against her. Unable to peer too far ahead in the dark, and hardly able to breathe, she looked back to see the three wolves gaining quickly. Jessica looked again in front to see a giant silhouetted creature running toward her through the thick, gusty winds. She could only imagine it was the leader that had made his way around to cut off her escape. She tripped and fell to the ground. Then the creature leaped into the air, breaking through the dusty haze. It could only be described as a giant snow leopard.

Soon it became clear that its target wasn't Jessica, but the wolves. With a loud roar it grabbed a wolf by the scruff of its neck, tossing it aside. The creature then thrashed the second wolf, making quick work of the two. In the heat of battle, the third wolf yelped, and other wolves emerged to its aid. Jessica made her way to her feet and kept running without looking back to see what became of her mysterious savior.

After days of wandering and, on the edge of malnutrition, she made it to the city limits. She was found by kind strangers, who delivered her to Grace General Hospital. From that day on, she lacked for nothing. Her "miserly" parents had left her a vast trust fund. She applied herself to her academics, earning her doctorate by the age of seventeen.

A Winter In The Wilderness: Why We Need Untamed Animals was the title of Dr. Jessica Winter's groundbreaking zoology dissertation calling for more research and the preservation of animals.

Jessica made yearly pilgrimages to where her parents died, and she wished to continue with the practice. She worked with the animal preserve, who happily footed the bill for the trips and sent a small crew of eager interns and specialists to accompany the renowned zoologist. Although Jessica was fairly savvy, she was slowly being entangled in the several strings attached to the agreement. The preserve's board hoped she would find the larger dominant animals, like the kind that she claimed saved her life. The board placed many resources at her disposal and appointed the well-connected Mr. Hawthorne to be her advisor. The yearly journey was not without peril or casualties, and was not for the faint of heart.

In the wilderness, you don't find the animals; they find you. The trips proved unfruitful, and the board of directors threatened to cut her grant. She marshaled her considerable financial forces and drained her own estate in an attempt at a hostile takeover of S-CAP. The pursuit ended in a stalemate, granting her the title of managing director. Yet the position lacked the teeth of resources and social ties truly needed to enact real change. The preserve was not a profitable investment. It didn't take long for her to become buried in a mountain of responsibilities, and a few years passed before her next journey into the wilderness. A number of shady backroom deals with various officials, including, and most regrettably, a deal with Leonardo, were a constant cause of concern to Ms. Winters.

But on her next trip, she discovered a rather large lioness. Jessica named her Teresa. It was with much fanfare that the district backed Jessica with marketing dollars and the like, hoping this would bring a much-needed economic boom to the district. With Leonardo holding a large portion of Jessica's debt, it gave him the in he was looking for to get some recognition for South Central's revitalization hopes.

There was something about Jessica, a certain irresistible quality. It wasn't long before Leonardo had taken an obsessive interest in her. The line between a power grab and wanting to own Jessica at the cost of everything else became blurred.

With her identity tied up in saving the animals, Jessica had resolved to offer herself up sacrificially to gain a research platform, a debt-free slate, and full control of the preserve. These plans were thwarted by her encounter with Daniel.

With the wild incident looming in the public's mind and the sudden disappearance of her prize catch, it would only be a matter of time before the vested parties started calling in their markers.

Jessica stopped her exercise regimen a bit short to look at the gash on her forearm. Her routine had caused it to become aggravated, and she made her way to the bathroom to redress the wound.

"Now what am I going to do?" she remarked, hoping an inner voice would help her determine her next move.

CHAPTER 10

ORPHANS

"This is torture," Daniel thought as he exited the glass doors of a local store. It was a one-story red brick building with a whitewashed tin roof, and it occupied the entire block. He paused for a moment to look up at the large sign resting atop the building. The dirty white sign was oval shaped and stood five- feet tall and three feet thick; it slowly swiveled on a pole that was just as thick. It read "South Central Meat Market" in red relief letters. In cursive relief just below, it read "GMO Meats of All Flavors."

It was almost two weeks since Teresa had found him in the tunnels, and now Daniel was toughing it out as the sole provider for another living thing. They lived off whatever he could scrape together. Most of what he earned from his portrait drawing in the park went toward feeding the feline. The plastic bags of red flesh hung heavily from Daniel's hands, making his palms raw.

He then spotted a talkie booth, just to the side of the building. It was a nine-foot-tall wooden box with chipped blue paint and many coiled metal antennae fastened to the top. The yellow "talkie" logo—a circle bracketed by three semicircles—was imprinted on the side. The door to the talkie booth was missing, but the area around the meat market was isolated, and Daniel wasn't too worried about privacy. He walked over to the booth and struggled to keep hold of the groceries while attempting to make the call.

"Hey, Jessica, it's me. Daniel. Uh, you would not guess what happened to me on the way home the other day. Call me...actually, I might have to just try calling you again since I don't have a talkie. Okay, talk soon."

It was similar to the other messages he'd left since Teresa appeared. He supposed that Jessica would want her back, but didn't think she'd want him leaving messages about it on her machine.

As he left the booth, he found a gang of boys loitering nearby.

"Hey, little man, going to a cookout? Can we come?" the leader taunted.

Daniel gripped the bags and walked away hurriedly as they laughed. He was sure that commanding Teresa to bite people he didn't like wasn't a real solution to any of his problems. But on occasions like this, the thought did cross his mind.

Daniel arrived at a secluded underground spot to serve up an early evening meal. The sight of her eating made him queasy. Even after whatever had happened that night, he still did not desire to eat meat.

Afterward, he worked to sharpen their communication skills. Daniel was inclined to use words, while she used various growling tones, but their true messages were understood and interpreted nonverbally in most cases. Daniel enjoyed having a companion. He had a sense that she was somehow at his command, albeit in an argumentative and stubborn manner.

"For such a tough, overgrown cat, you spend all your time lying around and eating meat all day," he teased Teresa with a big smile; she ignored him. "Who's the servant in this setup anyway?" Daniel said, and as he moved closer, she nipped at him playfully, not making contact. "Just you wait until I get Jessica," he warned.

Yet so many days had passed, and Daniel was increasingly plagued by the notion that Jessica no longer wanted anything to do with him.

A few days later, as he wandered the marketplace of South Central, Daniel heard an announcement through a barely functioning mounted speaker: a call for all artists interested in the South Central Animal Preserve's contest to attend a special briefing at the outdoor auditorium in the park.

The amphitheater was an open concrete slab floor underneath a sparse cover provided by five famished trees. The area was about seven hundred square feet, the ground cracked and under heavy disrepair. Neon-yellow fencing quartered off areas along the edges, warning parents that it was not safe for their little ones. The stage looked just as precarious; the brick-laid quarter-dome structure was splintered and had noticeably loose bricks at its height.

Daniel wore his dark-brown sweater zipped up in the front with the hood covering his low-hanging head. Unlike most of his peers, he arrived empty-handed, and kept his hands in his pocket. His outfit blended well with those of the other attendees, who were mostly Commoners.

There were no seats or benches. As the enormous brood of young artists began to pile in, squatting room filled up quickly, and those toward the back were required to stand. Each artist carried either small cases for his or her work or large folios containing life-sized renderings. Some looked around and up at the sky, passing the time in contemplation, while others quickly found friends and gathered in small clusters to share a cigarette or a flask, and a few laughs. There were a couple groups where Commoners comingled with vampires, it was a rare sight. Such "repentant" vampires carried themselves in a different manner from the rest, and, despite regular relapses, the company of Commoners was a risk that both repentants and some Commoners were willing to take to attain a sense of community on the fringes of society.

Naturally, there were several students from Central Arts Tech, which was the trade school to attend when seriously considering making a living in the arts. These students wore telltale navy-blue jackets with the school's crest—a shield with the overlapping letters C, A, and T—sewn onto the jacket pocket. Daniel could hear snippets of their conversation.

"Valese was a god. If only I had one ounce of his talent," said one student to his peers, and the rest nodded.

The wait dragged on as four assistants wearing bright-blue badges occupied the stage, but without any authority to speak up or address the crowd; they fumbled with clipboards, checked their watches, and attempted to avoid making prolonged eye contact with the audience.

After almost an hour, the volume of mumbled conversations swelled. Then Mr. Hawthorne made his way to the stage. Unlike the slumped, self-conscious stances of his assistants, he strode on the stage fully upright and unflinching. His skin was almost white, and his radiant three-piece suit was the brightest object in sight. Yet most of the audience did not make quick notice of his presence. Daniel looked at the area around the stage and its side exits. Jessica was nowhere to be seen.

"Vampire poser," grumbled someone standing close to Daniel.

An assistant handed Mr. Hawthorne a bullhorn. He held it in the air, pressing the siren. The sudden loud sound and the ringing that followed pierced their chatter. A few, especially Daniel, struggled to overcome the disorienting aftereffect. Mr. Hawthorne took a clipboard from the assistant who had the displeasure of being at close range for the sonic blast. After gaining their attention, he lackadaisically reviewed the notes and then began to read his address verbatim in a tone void of any emotion. He spoke into the bullhorn.

"The South Central Animal Preserve is a rare treasure in our district, and should be a source of pride for all Anthrazitites. For years, we've worked tirelessly to restore its reputation..."

A few mumbled voices rose from the listeners, and he raised his voice with precision enough to cover them exactly.

"For excellence. We sincerely hope to be a top-class attraction once more for the entire city and a boon to our local community. However, at this time, due to the ongoing investigation and concerns for public safety, we regret to inform you that our much-anticipated resident artist contest has been postponed indefinitely."

The crowd let out a unified response of shock and dismay. The grumbling began, and Jessica's advisor waited all of thirty seconds before continuing his staid news delivery.

"S-CAP and Ms. Jessica Winters offer our sincerest apologies. She urges you not to give up on your craft.

The board of directors continues to work tirelessly with the city to provide opportunities for all. We offer our sincerest thanks to the Drake family for their undying pledge to sustain and preserve Anthrazit, today and always. Thank you, everyone and..." He paused briefly, looked up from the page, and shrugged. "Good luck."

With that, he marched off the stage, tailed by his assistants.

The crowd erupted in chaotic noise. What were before mumbled conversations, mixtures of anxiety, and excitement, turned into angry yelling, weeping, and bewildered utterances. The mixture of emotion cut across both Commoner and vampire applicant hopefuls. A pale-skinned young man wearing all black standing several feet away, an obvious vampire, had redness in his cheeks and an angered stare. He took the strap of his folio from his shoulder and, with superhuman strength, ripped the leather case in half, threw it on the ground, and stormed off, pushing others out of the way.

"What do you mean, what am I going to do now?" said a girl from behind Daniel. He swiveled to notice that she was on her mini talkie, most likely talking to a parent or guardian. "This was it; there is no backup plan," she cried.

"Unbelievable," muttered a voice.

"Aren't you going to even look at all the work we put in?" yelled another young man; his friends held him back from charging the stage.

Some walked away, leaving their works behind. There were a few renderings that easily bested Daniel's talent, but they were quickly tattered and trampled. Someone threw a glass bottle at the stage, and it shattered against the back wall. Police officers began to move in as less-riotous personalities, including Daniel, quietly migrated away from the scene. Looking over his shoulder, he saw a few who were livid enough to get physical with the officers. He ducked his head and avoided eye contact.

Despite the brewing unrest, Daniel was not ready to leave the preserve's grounds. Walking into the main office building was probably too brazen—the security detail there was sure to be keen. But it wouldn't hurt to survey Teresa's old den. Maybe Jessica would be there too.

The den was still crawling with special inspectors, who were searching for more clues to Teresa's disappearance. The inspectors wore dark-red jackets and bright-yellow surgical gloves. Most had ghostly pale skin. Daniel stood behind a small group of spectators who looked on from behind the exhibit's fence as the inspectors performed their duties.

They even had a hellhound with them—a four-foot-high canine beast with acute smell and hearing. These creatures were a result of the Drake family's attempts to create a cure for the dying animals, using their vampire DNA.

The hound looked at the crowd with a menacing expression. It spotted Daniel and bared its large fangs, as well as several other teeth that were just as overgrown. Some cheered, taking the hound's posturing as a part of the spectacle, but Daniel realized that he was vulnerable and quickly walked away. Had his cover been blown?

From that point on, it seemed that every vampire was staring him down. From street to street, each one locked eyes with him. Businessmen in a hurried pace would turn their heads to follow his trail, and attractive women in close conversation would break off to look at him, some changing to reveal the ruined face of Nosferatu. If any of them had been appointed to locate Daniel, he was positive that he wouldn't stand a chance.

Clunk! A big rock hit him in the back of the head.

"Ha-ha!" a preteen vampire boy taunted, and his Commoner friends laughed.

They began picking up more stones. Daniel ducked into the local hostel as quickly as he could and locked the door behind him. The loud sound of rocks pelting the door could be heard from the other side. There was the janitor mopping the floors of the shabby interior.

"Friends, always playing around," Daniel joked, hoping to buy some time.

"I'll give you five minutes," the janitor said and continued to mop.

━━╪╌ ╌╪━━

Later that evening, Daniel sat in the back pew of the parish. With his hands clasped, he prayed. He didn't want to return under these conditions again, but it seemed he had nowhere else to hide. Daniel sat shaken, and prayed desperately.

"Are you up there? I could use a little help. Just make it stop. I am nothing, yet everything is turning against me. I can see them coming. Leonardo and his monsters are just waiting to get me. Please let them take me, convert me, and use me. At least my torture will end."

"So you're back." The voice was unmistakable.

"Father Frank," Daniel replied and stood up.

"This place is meant for many things, none of which include hiding."

"Please, let me stay. Just for a couple of days. They won't come in here." There was no response. Daniel went on. "I was wrong. I shouldn't have said the things I did. I was angry...and stupid," he begged.

"Daniel, you need to leave." Father Frank began to walk away.

"I'm homeless!"

Father Frank stopped in his tracks, and Daniel continued. "I lost my room at the hostel, and I've been living in the sewers. Please."

The priest turned and looked at him, at first surprised, but then his brow relaxed.

122

"Daniel, you've got to be the most stubborn, helpless thing I know."

"Why me? Why are they after me?"

"Creatures of prey always seek out the weakest of the herd," Father Frank replied clinically. "I'll get you some blankets."

He made his way to the spiral staircase and began his ascent.

⚞ ⚟

Jessica Winters was rarely backed into a corner. But there she was. The large glass windows of her office overlooked a dimly lit walking path outside. Jessica looked at the path with longing, thinking of how quickly the darkness had come.

"The inspectors have finished their investigation." The voice was that of Mr. Hawthorne as he stood in the doorway, his hands folded behind his back.

"Thank you, Mr. Hawthorne. That is good news. Their presence had become a disruption to the tours."

Her office was surprisingly small for a person of her position, but she had so many books, papers, and loose clutter lying around that it made the space shrink even further.

"You'll be happy to know that you've been cleared of any wrongdoing in Teresa's disappearance," said Mr. Hawthorne.

"Was there ever any doubt?" Jessica asked with a dose of sarcasm.

"How did you get that nasty gash on your arm again?"

"I was doing some inspecting of my own. I wanted to see Teresa's cave and carelessly cut myself on the service-entrance fence."

"And then there is the matter of the over-mobile," he continued.

"What about it?" she replied.

"They are a serviceperson's transport, for heavy loads and deliveries, yet security spotted you leaving the premises in one that very night."

"As you are well aware, and as I told the inspectors, the lease for my mobile expired, and I'm still deciding on my next one. That night I just needed a way to get home. My residence can attest to the fact that it was parked in the garage all night. I returned it the very next morning."

"Washed and detailed," he added. "A woman of your accomplishments should have her own mobile. Owning one is not a replacement for your memories of your parents," Mr. Hawthorne replied astutely.

"Is this matter closed, or not?" Jessica replied sharply.

Mr. Hawthorne drummed his nails on the doorframe. "You may be the operational owner of the preserve, but you are still accountable to the board of trustees. We simply cannot ignore infractions of this manner. The facilities and service mobiles cannot be used for personal matters."

"It will not happen again. Now as you can see, there are several matters I need to attend to. I'm sure the board would appreciate my diligence in executing my duties."

"And research."

"Research?" She raised her eyebrows.

"Well, with your catch now vanished, we would be willing to fund another…pilgrimage. I'm sure you of all people are eager to find a replacement."

"Absolutely." She stood a little more upright and straightened the jacket of her suit by tugging on the ends. "I'll begin drafting a plan and outline a schedule."

Mr. Hawthorne left and closed the door quietly behind him. She quickly grabbed her chair and threw herself into it, wondering how long she could keep this up.

Leonardo was the youngest of the over fifty pure blood vampires in the Drake family—a true blood descendant of Prime Minister Drake. To him, that meant he was a step above the "yes" fangs, but was not treated as an equal by his siblings. According to his older siblings, he lacked the sangfroid discipline necessary to respectably carry on the bloodline. He had in fact been marginalized by his brothers and sisters as an unruly brat and had been completely invisible to his father, the prime minister.

Less than a decade after settling into their positions of rule, the fifteen governing children had successfully distilled their absent father's canon into the sublime tenets of superior governing. They accepted their father's departure as the final object lesson. Hardly anyone saw them, yet their prominence in the thoughts of Commoners made them ubiquitous. When the siblings did gather for a feast, Leonardo seemed to discover the event only after it had passed. He soon despised the thought of them and realized it was up to him if he wanted to rule.

Leonardo wanted to prove his significance in such a magnificent way that his father would have to come back just to make note of it. Being on the outs with almost everyone placed him a long way off from his goal, though. After much jockeying and a strong role in suppressing the uprising, he was granted control of South Central District. It was a struggling district—almost an insult, really.

Still, one could argue that Leonardo was a man who had everything. He was the youngest to run his own district. Unlike his siblings, he was involved in the nitty-gritty of district life. When a Nosferatu was inducted, he threw the biggest feasting parties. He was notorious for popping into business meetings to inject his outlandish ideas, however counterproductive they might be.

Many of his siblings opted for long periods of meditation in confined spaces and small rooms. An extreme sect arose that touted the benefits of prolonged rest in coffins. However, it was not uncommon to spot Leonardo, accompanied by his top advisers, making his way through the market corridors and sampling the goods as a part of "quality control." He also enjoyed driving around South Central in his signature red mobile.

Throwing Daniel into the lion's pit was supposed to be funny and somewhat poetic, Leonardo thought. Daniel was not the first one who Leonardo had desired to make an example of, but he was the only one to have survived. This made Leonardo despise him all the more.

⇒⊹⊹⊱

On this night, Leonardo got word through his eyes and ears on the street that Daniel was hiding out in the local parish. Despite the canon's warning to stay away from the sacred places of the unturned, Leonardo headed toward the parish. He looked forward to facing Daniel. He just needed to blow off a little steam.

Leonardo arrived in front of the church at that strange time that neither night nor morning cared to claim as its own. He was driving his lavish red mobile with gold-plated trimmings and pipes. He parked right by the steps. There were a couple of large drone vampires awaiting him at the rendezvous.

"Is he still in there?" Leonardo asked.

One of the drones nodded in response. A handful of vampires and Commoners stood at the street corners, waiting eagerly like kids at a schoolyard brawl.

Leonardo stepped out of his mobile and adjusted his leather jacket. He sat on the long hood, puffing up his chest, and then reached into his pocket and pulled out a cigarette. He ran his hand through his slicked hair and itched behind his ear. A couple of the onlookers began to chant.

"Come out, bitch!" someone yelled.

The doors of the church creaked open slightly, and Father Frank stepped out. The cold, blue street lamps threw a spotlight on him. The crowd became deathly quiet.

"Okay, everybody, it's really late. I'm sure Governor Leonardo," he glanced toward Leonardo, "would prefer that you go about your business, rather than spending a day or two in jail for breaking the sanctuary premises laws. So let's sleep this one off, shall we?" He turned and reached for the door.

"What do you know about our rules?" someone yelled, and the ruckus started up again.

Leonardo kicked the steps in front of him so hard that the concrete cracked. The foundation of the church shuddered.

Father Frank just made it inside and began to address Daniel. "It's only a few more hours until daybreak. They always get worked up in the late-night hours. Vampires…"

A large, jagged fragment of concrete crashed through the church's massive stained-glass window. The colorful pieces rained down on Father Frank as the chunk struck him in the head. He dropped limply to the ground. Blood poured out from his skull, coating the shards of colorful glass crimson.

"Father Frank!"

Daniel ran to his side and rolled him over, scooping him into his arms. Father Frank reached up to touch his face, and Daniel started to cry. There was a low, rumbling sound from high above them.

"Though you aren't mine, you are the best child I could have hoped for." With a sigh, Father Frank breathed his last.

Daniel was filled with rage. He stood up and walked with long, determined strides toward the doors, grabbing a tall candle stand along the way. It took effort, but he pulled the doors open and charged through the entryway.

"You want to fight? Here I am—come and get me!" Daniel's eyes began to glow.

A drone stepped up to face Daniel on the steps of the plaza. Daniel ducked the vampire's first swing, and swung the candle stand at his opponent. The drone grabbed the heavy metal bar and swung Daniel into one of the parish's pillars. He turned to the spectators, throwing his hand in the air like a gladiator in a grand coliseum. Everyone cheered. Although it wasn't wise,

Daniel pulled himself to his feet. The drone turned, realizing that Daniel didn't plan to accept defeat so easily. He looked to Leonardo for instruction. Leonardo stuck out his hand and gave a thumbs down. The crowd cheered as the colossal vampire prepared to carry out the finish.

At that moment, there was a cracking and shifting sound. It came from the roof of the church. The huge stone gargoyle that had adorned the façade came crashing down on the drone.

What terrible luck had loosened the statue at just the right moment? The crowd murmured, and then someone screamed. The statue stood. It stepped toward Daniel, kneeling to look at the scrawny youth. It reached out and took the griffin pendant in its hand. The griffin was inscribed with a two-syllable phrase from which Father Frank had derived Daniel's name.

"Da Il," the gargoyle read reverently.

He held Daniel's face in his coarse, three-fingered hand, looking from the boy's blue to his hazel eye. With a weary smile, he nodded.

A large vampire loomed over the gargoyle's shoulder, but the statue swiftly spun around and landed a right hook that sent his opponent clear across the street and through a storefront. The gargoyle stood up to his full height, easily head and shoulders above the drones. He then extended his massive stone wings, flexed his chiseled biceps, and growled. The small crowd panicked, and one or two bared their fangs. Most scampered away. Leonardo furrowed his eyebrows but stood his ground. Sirens blared, announcing that the police mobiles were on their way.

Daniel began to head back into the parish, but the stone gargoyle bent down, scooped him up, and tossed him over his shoulder.

"Let me go! Father Frank," Daniel screamed as the gargoyle ran off with loud stomps, and faded out of sight.

CHAPTER 11
LOVED

It was almost 5:00 a.m. Daniel sat seemingly alone on the platform of the amphitheater, emotionally drained; there were no tears left to continue crying. The thunder had carried on into the morning but had produced nothing and eventually faded. The gargoyle stepped out from the shadows of the quarter-dome structure to stand behind Daniel.

"Da Il, sir. We should keep moving. I'm sure there will be a search party," he advised, but Daniel did not budge. The gargoyle looked at his hands and touched the stony surface of his forearm and shoulders, bewildered by his own form.

"Who are you? What are you?" Daniel finally spoke, as he stood to face the giant.

At first the gargoyle stretched out his arm to greet Daniel in a familial manner, but when Daniel did not reciprocate, he snapped to attention.

"Xi." (It sounded like "T-see.")

"Chee?"

"Xi, sir. Captain of the royal gargoyle armies," he replied without moving, as Daniel poked at the creature's arm.

There was no give. The rough gravel surface was all one solid piece. Daniel attempted to lift its wrist using both of his hands. The gargoyle moved voluntarily to appease his curiosity. As he moved the joints in his fingers, the stone broke and fractured in those places and then "healed" quickly to the masonry's new position. The staccato rhythm to his motion became more noticeable.

"Xi, what armies are you talking about?"

"Sir, may I suggest that we find some other place? We are not quite out of danger here."

Daniel shook his head. "Why are you here?"

Xi realized that the sad young man had no memory at all. "Da Il, the last I—"

"Call me Daniel. Father Frank named me Daniel. That is my name."

Xi nodded gently. "Of course, sir. I had you in my arms. I thought we were safe, and then—"

"And then what?" Daniel responded.

"Something happened. I don't understand it. But this place, these buildings, all this wasn't here," the gargoyle replied pensively. He stepped closer to Daniel.

"You are so much older now, and not quite the way I imagined you'd turn out. It seems like only yesterday, Daniel." Xi knelt. "How would you feel if I told you that you were not abandoned, but dearly loved? How would it change your life if I told you that you are the son of a king?"

Daniel looked up at Xi, and the creature responded with a somber grin. The words were like a certain magic, promising a change—a new beginning. But the scruffy-haired young man reserved his reaction. Who could tell what was true?

"If I am the son of a king, that would change everything," Daniel thought.

A siren screeched loudly in the distance.

"I will tell you everything, I promise. But we have to go," Xi pleaded.

Daniel looked around at the grounds surrounding the amphitheater. Many portfolios and sketchbooks still littered the area. Daniel jumped down from the stage and grabbed a shoulder bag. He quickly sifted through tossed sketchbooks, finding one with mostly unused pages, and tossed it into the bag. He ran toward a heavily thicketed area on the other side of the square.

"Follow me!" Daniel called out.

"You are your father's son," Xi muttered. He stepped down from the stage and chased after Daniel.

They made their way through a secluded copse of rotted trees. The gargoyle was surprised to see how quickly the tree limbs crumbled—they dissolved with the slightest touch.

"Do you believe in the gods?" Xi asked.

"I believe there is one God, and that our lives are controlled by something higher than ourselves. It's the way I was raised." He glanced at Xi, and then added, "I believe as much as anyone can in a place as messed up as this."

"Dark days indeed," Xi replied. "I'm sorry for the death of your clergyman. A king should always have strength on his left and spiritual wisdom on his right."

Daniel stopped and looked at Xi.

"It's an old proverb. Wisdom should be on the right, because it is of greater power than physical strength."

"He deserved better," said Daniel. "We shouldn't have left him."

Xi sighed and hung his head.

When they approached a steep embankment, the two made their way down cautiously.

"Those creatures—have they always been here?"

"You mean the vampires. I think they have been in Anthrazit as long as anyone else, but they only started ruling since the Drake family took over. The Family monopolizes just about everything. Getting turned is the only way to really get ahead."

"We should lie low for a little while," Xi started. "Then we need to find our way back to the kingdom. I've just got to find out how to get there."

"We can probably start by using the backstreets—they're less conspicuous. There are a few intersections that will be difficult to cross without drawing some attention. The best route is to cross that incline up ahead."

Daniel pointed in the direction he spoke of, but then paused and took a seat on a rocky ledge.

"Just give me a minute."

He cupped both hands above his forehead, stifling a sob.

CHAPTER 12
FAMILY

The east side of Central District was a cold place. The frigid air bit at the skin, even under five layers of clothing. In this district, all knew their places. After the morning rush, there weren't many pedestrians left to crowd the streets, and few paused to admire the grand stone architecture, even though the buildings easily dwarfed anything in South Central.

The major landmark of this section of Central was Alpha Aion Cathedral, which could be seen from a long way off. The landmark cathedral occupied four square blocks and was ten stories taller than the largest thing in the district. Leonardo's red mobile pulled up in front and double parked. He revved the engines, releasing a plume of coal dust, and then turned the ignition key, ceasing the loud racket. The drone vampire guards posted at the grand, column-lined entrance reacted with a frown and a snarl but took no action. It had been some time since his last visit, but they knew to whose family he belonged.

The grand cathedral maintained its religious outer shell, but Drake's descendants had long ago worked around the limitation on their ability to stand in church. They simply turned the controlling members of the grand institution, corrupting the church from the inside.

Deep within, there was a chamber with jagged walls leading all the way up to a skylight several stories above. The room was large, round, and dimly lit by torches fastened to the walls at even intervals. There were also unlit passages that led out of the room, and each had a pair of guards standing watch.

Drawn on the floor in the center of the room was a labyrinth, and upon it a man paced, following, stopping, and turning as the lines instructed. It was the dark priest, Aitalas, appointed guardian of the Drake estate. His black silk robes flowed and twisted with every move.

He continued to pace, even as the silence was interrupted by loud footsteps coming from the main entry to the chamber. Leonardo marched toward him and stepped across the edge of the labyrinth. The priest stopped and glared over his shoulder at Leonardo, who stopped and backpedaled enough to stand just outside the markings.

A close look at the priest revealed aged bite marks in the wrinkled skin of his neck.

"You summoned, and I obeyed, but I could have easily accepted your directions in a talkie message. Technology can be quite useful," said Leonardo impatiently.

"Are all creatures doomed to fall?" the priest asked after a long delay. He interrupted his labyrinth ritual and now walked over to Leonardo as if the lines were nonexistent. "Answer me, Leonardo," he said, staring at him with menacing, glowing eyes.

"Not all. We are superior," Leonardo answered smugly.

The priest quickly struck him across the face with a right backhand. A red welt appeared on Leonardo's cheek, and he gently touched the tender spot. It hurt.

The priest removed his long black gloves to reveal a crimson signet ring on his ring finger, which caused the welt. He began pacing his labyrinth once more.

"There are so many paths to a fall: pride, lust, greed, blind ambition. Surprisingly, you desire to walk them all simultaneously," said the priest. His voice boiled with disappointment and anger. He calmed himself and took a breath. "The buildings you destroyed at the edge of South Central—it's time you rebuilt them."

"Why? It's a monument to the defeat of the infidels," Leonardo rebutted.

"At first they will fear you, but fear can breed a special brand of rage that topples the largest of kingdoms."

"After we broke through their defenses, what did my brothers and sisters find? More magical creatures like the ones in our study books?" Leonardo asked.

"Leave it be. Nothing good will come from such curiosity. We dissuade the Commoners from such beliefs with good reason, you know. Leave those matters to your siblings. The only magic you need to be concerned with is that which we can already control – that adds to the power of this house. You must only concern yourself with what you have been given and not to be under the power of another," the priest replied as he marveled at the ring on his finger. "Speaking of which, why are you so obsessed with this woman and anyone who comes close to her? She is not even a woman," he said, with a flippant backhanded gesture, "but a child wearing grownup clothes."

"I would have turned her," Leonardo replied.

"Master already gave you your share."

"My teeth were already in her neck," Leonardo retorted.

"She was not yours!" the priest barked in an unnatural, monstrous voice.

Leonardo was silent for a moment.

"I wouldn't expect a servant to understand," Leonardo said under his breath, just loud enough to bait the priest.

But Aitalas was wiser than to get caught up in a petty squabble.

"Master claimed this city. It took him lifetimes. Super strength and immortality weren't enough—it took blood and sweat to build this empire. I was fortunate to be one of the first he turned, long before he had any offspring. After demonstrating my unwavering faithfulness, he entrusted me with the signet ring and oversight of this region. Purebred you are, but also one of, what, hundreds? We stopped counting after a while. You are certainly among the least capable."

Leonardo shuffled his weight under the scolding.

"Poor Leonardo. You think you deserve more."

"South Central is a dump. I hate that place! If I could only get Father's attention. I have the perfect opportunity now." Leonardo looked up, holding Aitalas's gaze with his own. "I have found a magical creature. One made of stone, one that has decided to reveal itself to just about everyone in South Central. I intend to take him down. I just need a couple tools. An enchanted stone or a magic-powered mechanical would be great for starters."

The priest raised an eyebrow and then looked over his shoulder at a figure covered in a cloak knelt at a small altar made out of beaten metal.

"What were the circumstances?" he asked.

"I was messing with this kid: Doug, Danny, or something. He's a nobody. I don't even want him as a lackey. Just the sight of him makes me..." He shivered and shook his hands like a schoolboy avoiding playground germs. "Anyway, out of nowhere, this statue just jumped out and took out my biggest drones."

"So this boy, as you say, attracted a magical creature to guard him, and you are not even curious as to why. There are very few magicals left, and it didn't pique your curiosity?" The dark priest began to yell. "Good grief! I must have done something wrong raising you."

"Does that mean you'll help me? This is my big shot to impress Dad."

"How do you expect to impress him when we can't even find him?" Aitalas crossed his arms. "Tell you what…I'll make the call. Find this boy and any magical creatures that may be consorting with him. Kill them all. Do not attempt to turn them. Remember what happened to Anthony during the uprising."

"There's no way he's hiding a magical weapon; the coward would have tried to use it by now," Leonardo replied. "It will be done even if I have to tear the district apart to do it," he continued with absolute resolution.

"And Jessica Winters as well," the priest added.

Leonardo paused. "Fine," he conceded.

"And since you have proven incapable of handling your own affairs," the priest said, gesturing toward the figure kneeling at the altar.

The figure rose, and Leonardo could tell by the slender, seductive, fluid shape that it was a woman.

She wore high-heeled, patent-leather boots. Her hooded cloak was a deep-crimson red with sleeves rolled up past her elbows and held in place by large buckles. Her forearms were wrapped in gray bandages, although her hands were free. Under her cloak, she wore tight-fitting black lace.

"Phoenix?" Leonardo couldn't believe his eyes.

"Hello, brother."

Phoenix had a dark, smoky voice. She removed her hood to reveal black hair with a bluish sheen. Her eyes were ice-white with a blue halo, and she wore dark liner along their edges. Her dark-red lips had two piercings to the left, and she had a small stud nose ring to top it off.

Leonardo gave an incredulous look.

"I'm back in the fold," she said.

Her hips swayed gently, and the cloak floated back as she walked, revealing vertically stacked, double-barreled pistols strapped to her hips.

"I find that hard to believe. Those gray bandages aren't going to fool anyone."

"Penance scars don't go away, you know that. It's better to keep them hidden. But I'm no longer practicing abstinence—that's what matters. When my thirst arises, I fulfill it. Just like anyone else."

Leonardo stepped in close and grabbed her by the cheeks. "Those fangs are chipped but growing back nicely," he growled.

She pulled her head back and slapped his hand away.

"Touch me again, and I will sever those fingers before you can blink."

Leonardo shrugged. "Priest, you were so angry when she filed down her fangs. Remember?"

"Your sister has abandoned her religious folly and has returned to the assassin sect," Aitalas chided. "You would not have taken South Central without her, or have you so quickly forgotten?"

"It was right after that when she decided that she needed to 'find her soul.'" He scoffed. "No, I don't need her help. I want to do this on my own."

"You owe her your rule, and you must admit that she has been quite useful since her return. Haven't you noticed the disappearance of your most influential dissenters?"

A pair of slender vampires emerged from the shadows on either side of the chamber, a man and a woman, dressed similarly to Phoenix. They joined the siblings and the priest.

The priest motioned to a pair of column guards, sharply clapping his raised hands. The guards headed into a dark entryway just behind them. "A small peace offering is coming. This is an opportunity for you both to prove your worth," said the priest.

The two guards emerged with a young woman in a simple white dress, her wrists bound by a rope. The guards carried her by the elbows, and she kicked and screamed at them. Finally, they lifted her until her feet barely touched the ground.

They tossed her in the middle of the labyrinth, where the young woman fell to her knees. Phoenix, Leonardo, and the priest encircled her. Phoenix stooped down and sniffed the woman's dark-brown hair.

"Mmm...virgin. My favorite," said Phoenix.

She bit the woman's neck with such voraciousness that her head was almost completely torn off. Leonardo joined in. The two assassins looked to the priest for permission, hoping for a taste. He nodded, giving his consent. They kneeled down to lick the floor of the labyrinth, which was covered in the woman's blood.

After the meal was complete, the two sat like children, propped up against the wall. Leonardo licked his blood-soaked fingers. "This is just like the time we caught that caravan coming out of the South Expressways." He giggled. "No wonder travelers never venture into Anthrazit anymore."

"Oh, no, that was much better. There was more for everybody," said Phoenix.

"Well, I'm not complaining." Leonardo chuckled.

Phoenix gave him a big grin and stood up. "I should wash up before we head out," she said, and headed into one of the halls to find the nearest lavatory.

It was a small, cramped space. She closed the door behind her. After leaning against the door, she stuck her index finger deep inside her mouth. She gagged and fell to the ground. She knelt and hugged the porcelain bowl close like a lover and let the bloody vomit flow. The whole time, Phoenix convulsed, but kept her head down, not wanting to spill or add more to the clean-up that was sure to follow.

She fell to her bottom and wiped her mouth on the bandages. Partially shivering, she frantically unwrapped one of the bandages and pulled out a knife from a back pocket. It was a silver blade, finely etched with elaborate symbols.

She stabbed and sliced away at her forearm, but there was no blood, just areas of crusted ash. She prayed.

"Forgive me. If there is a God, please hear me. Replace my heart of ashes with a heart of flesh. Have mercy on me and redeem my lost soul." She then placed her hands on her head, trying to feel something.

She finally appeared back in the chamber, with hurried strides.

"Man, that took a long time. A woman thing?" Leonardo taunted.

"Funny. Okay, let's go."

She walked right past him, and the two assassins followed.

"So he has magical creatures with him? How many?"

Leonardo reluctantly followed. "Just one, I think."

CHAPTER 13
LETTING GO

"Are you ready?" Daniel asked, as he and Xi stood in the dark, narrow alley.

The gargoyle retracted his wings as much as possible, but they still scraped along the walls. The foot traffic had already started to build. They missed the time window to be less conspicuous, and rush hour was approaching.

"Is there no other way?" asked Xi. He was not in his element and hoped for a different strategy.

"Two streets ahead there are street grates that should be just big enough for you to make it through and into the sewers. Once we are down there, we can get anywhere in the district and beyond. This is the easiest entry in South Central, but we have to make it across this busy intersection," explained Daniel. "You have to really know your way around to survive in Anthrazit."

"Okay, let's go," said Xi, who was now committed.

They stepped out into the open and walked briskly down the sidewalk. Everyone's frenzied daily pace slowed to a crawl. The heads-down behavior ceased on a massive scale, and everyone gawked. Some looked at Daniel as he walked a bit ahead of the gargoyle, clearing a path, but most looked at Xi.

It started as merely hushed chatter, but the volume built to almost a feverish pitch within seconds.

Suddenly, a gentleman in the distance yelled, "Officer, Officer!" and pointed to the gargoyle. Two officers headed toward them. One got on his walkie-talkie, calling for some backup.

"Excuse me, pardon me. Let us through," said Daniel, and picked up the pace. Xi followed, hunching his shoulders.

There was the sound of a siren as a police mobile tried to make it through the crowded street, heading toward them. The police mobile siren blared, and a voice boomed from a megaphone. "Get out of the way!"

The crowd scattered, and soon Daniel and Xi were exposed.

"Follow me," Daniel said.

He turned at the street corner, and sprinted. Xi followed with footsteps that shook the ground. A large, grate-covered area was just across the next street, but a police mobile emerged from the around the corner and cut them off. Another one came behind them and blocked their escape.

Xi charged in front of Daniel and whipped around to smash his heavy tail against the police mobile's front hood. He then grabbed one of the doors, ripping it clean off. The officer was a Commoner and tried to hide on the floor of the police mobile. The gargoyle whirled like a discus thrower and hurled the car door at the other police mobile at the opposite end. The officer leaped out a split second before the rapidly rotating metal slammed into his mobile, cutting it in half.

"This way!" shouted Daniel.

He ran across the street and did his best to lift the heavy grate, but his puny arms couldn't make it budge. Xi came over and lifted the grate quickly, and they headed into the large opening.

They climbed down a worn-out metal ladder into a dark, two-story cavern. Partway down, the ladder gave way, and Daniel fell into the darkness. His fall was cushioned by a thick soup of raw sewage. Xi jumped down with a big splash that fully submerged Daniel.

"Ugh, gross," Daniel lamented. He resurfaced covered in chunky, slimy sewage.

"No, this is good. It should help cover our tracks."

Xi looked up as a few pedestrians looked down, trying to get another glimpse of what was sure to be the talk for the rest of the day.

"Let's keep moving."

After wading through liquid filth as deep as Daniel's kneecaps, the sewage levels began to recede.

"It is nice to have a bruiser on my side, for once," stated Daniel. He began making boxer jabs at an imaginary opponent. "The way you took out those guys was amazing. I'm so glad you're on my side."

Xi's expression changed slightly after hearing that, and he slowed his pace to allow Daniel to catch up. A few more exit points appeared.

"Just keep going straight ahead," said Daniel. "Actually, hang on a sec."

The creature stopped, and Daniel ran to the wall; it had several large pipes that ran down side by side from a closed grate high above.

"I kind of knew something like this would happen. It might sound weird," Daniel said. He began looking around on the ground. "But this is literally a dream come true. I've seen you, in my dreams. I was a little boy, and it was in a forest, and you weren't made of stone, so I guess the details aren't really the same." He picked up a large rock.

"What are you doing?" Xi asked.

"See these pipes? Most of them carry rot and sewage, but not this one."

Among the larger pipes, barely distinguishable except for its smaller size, was a much-thinner pipe. Daniel hit it a few times, and fresh water came gushing out. He washed as much of the sewage away as possible and drank liberally. The gargoyle washed off the larger areas of sewage as well.

"You are quite resourceful," Xi said. Then his lip twitched. "That was no dream. That was part of the journey when I rescued you."

"Was it my parents' idea?" asked Daniel.

"On your father's wishes. Your mother died during childbirth."

"What were they like? Tell me more about my parents." Daniel stood still and demanded. "My whole life I grew up thinking the worst of them. Please, I need to know the truth."

"When I heard your voice, I opened my eyes in this world for the first time. The first thing that struck me was that there is no sky. I bet you've never seen the sky," said the gargoyle.

Before them was a rather large ledge with a drop-off into unseen depths. Daniel sat on the ledge, and Xi joined him.

"It is clear; it is beautiful, the sky. I've only been awake in this world for a short time, and I already miss it. But I can still see it in my mind, endless in every direction. And the ground, lush and green, rising and descending with such vigor.

"On one side was the wall. It was like a fortress that ran along the border. That is where I lived, when I wasn't on duty. In the middle of the land stood a castle made of the purest white stone. It had amazing towers. There were many creatures of different kinds, and everyone lived in harmony with each other," said Xi as he reminisced.

Daniel stared at him with a puzzled expression, still awaiting the answer to his original question.

Xi sighed and continued. "All that belonged to your father, who was the best king we ever had. He was loving, genuine, and so wise. I think we could have expanded the kingdom a bit more, but your father didn't have an appetite for empire building. He used to stand on the balcony of the small west tower and gaze out on it all, completely still and lost in his thoughts. I couldn't see what he saw, but I think I do now."

"Why stand in a small tower? If I were king, I would throw the biggest parties in the biggest tower," Daniel interjected.

"It had been his room when he was younger, and he always liked that balcony."

"Did they have pointy ears like me?"

"Just about everyone does there. Did you see mine? I saw that Father Frank's ears weren't pointed—what a strange thing," Xi replied with a chuckle.

At that moment, Teresa came bounding out of one of the tunnels and leaped playfully on Daniel.

"Hey, there, girl. No matter where I am down here, you always find me, huh?" He stroked her back, and she purred like an incredibly overgrown kitten.

The gargoyle jumped back, astonished.

Daniel saw a chance to poke fun at his new protector. "Don't tell me a big creature like you is afraid of a—"

"A counterpart? You have a counterpart?"

"I'm not sure I would call us that, but let's just say we've kind of hugged it out," Daniel replied.

"Did you bite her?"

"Yes, and that was completely awkward and desperate."

"And took on the form of a beast?" Xi's voice was a rush.

Daniel frowned. "How did you know all that?"

"Well, then you've already completed the rite of passage!"

"What do you mean?"

The large stone creature knelt before Daniel, barely able to contain his excitement. "In the kingdom, boys and girls can pledge to join the feline Lyken warrior class. It takes years of training and study to prepare."

"What is a Lyken?" asked Daniel.

"Lykens are what you are, Daniel. Beings that look like this town's inhabitants, but have an inherited trait that allows them to bond with other creatures. The feline clan was the strongest and the most highly regarded," Xi explained. "Each pledge is required to bite and drink the blood of a beast without killing it. Then the pledge gains the strength of that beast and the ability to take that form. The most-skilled pledges are able to bond with the beast and make it a counterpart."

Daniel looked at the gargoyle, puzzled by all the new information.

"Daniel, do you know what this means?" Xi continued with great excitement.

Daniel stared, unsure of how to respond.

"To think you accomplished this without training, instruction, or study. Even without a pride."

"Without a pride?" Daniel asked.

"A group of peers who are deeply connected to each other," Gargoyle explained quickly. "Daniel, you were born to do something extraordinary. You are the lost prince, destined to restore the kingdom. It's in your blood."

Xi tapped Daniel on the chest. Daniel looked at the floor, trying to process these bold claims. It was one thing to have been the child of parents who did love him. But to be the prince of a kingdom with transforming beasts might be a bit much.

"This calls for a huge celebration!" Xi hoisted Daniel onto his shoulders and pranced around, letting out a series of joyful, grunting chants.

Despite being overwhelmed by the new circumstances and revelations, Daniel thought it was nice to have a companion, particularly one who seemed to know him better than he knew himself, and took such joy in everything about him.

"Wait, turn this way," Daniel said as Xi began to prance onward through the sewer.

Daniel laughed loudly as he basked in the joy of his newfound friend.

⇒+ +⇐

"I should just take her out," Leonardo said.

He was perched on a ledge in a secluded area of a railed mobile station, and was supporting a long-range sniper rifle complete with a scope. It was a serious weapon, complete with elaborately engraved symbols, custom made for one who considered killing an art form. Leonardo had a clear shot at Jessica, who was hard at work on her runner's platform.

"No!" Phoenix's voice rang out from the mini talkie in Leonardo's ear. "Just observe."

"Thanks for letting me borrow your piece, sis."

"Just don't scratch it. I expect to get it back just as I gave it to you."

"Have you located Daniel?" asked Leonardo.

"We're working on it; it might take a few days. Are you sure that's his name?" asked Phoenix.

"I think so. Don't tell me that not having a proper name will slow down your search. That doesn't say much about your tracking skills."

"Screw you. The girl is the perfect trap. Hold tight until we flush them out," Phoenix snapped.

"A trap, sounds delicious," said Leonardo as he licked his gold-capped fangs.

CHAPTER 14
LOST

Teresa tracked a little ahead of Xi, who kept Daniel on his shoulders. Daniel was noticeably quiet.

"I imagine you have lots more questions," Xi prodded.

"I grew up not thinking too much about where I came from even though I was so out of place. I thought if I was abandoned then no good could come from digging up the past. But now...I don't even know what to ask next."

"Well, now you know different, so ask away," Xi encouraged.

"So I was *supposed* to turn into that monster?" Daniel began.

"Not a monster," the gargoyle responded in mild rebuke. "It's a privilege to be able to take a form, a privilege that is earned."

"By biting an animal?"

"Not just any animal—the larger and stronger within their species. Your family and most in the kingdom preferred felines. This Teresa is a bit small, but she'll do."

Teresa turned and growled an objection.

"Eating meat makes me sick."

"Of course, Lyken beings only eat plants. Meat can be poisonous." Xi stopped and placed Daniel on the ground. "Okay, let's see it."

"See what?"

"Your beast form. Show it to me."

"Well, I'm not really sure how to do it on purpose. I only bit her because she bit me first. And then it all sort of...happened."

Teresa approached, and Daniel stooped to stroke her on the head. He then showed the scar from Teresa biting him in his side.

"That's a bit unorthodox," said Xi. "Still, I suppose we should get out of this city before anything else."

Daniel looked at the piped exit. After a little thought, he pointed. "Turn here."

"Have you started looking for a mate?" Xi asked lightly.

"A mate? Not really." Daniel released a geekish snort. "But there is one girl...woman," he self-corrected. "Jessica Winters. I can't seem to get my mind off her. She is way out of my league, though."

"An interest who is always in the heart and on one's mind. Young love. That is how it always starts," Xi replied. "Tell me all about her."

⋙ ⋘

Café Milo was closing up for the night. Jessica sat in a window seat, staring out into the growing dark. Her coffee was now cold and sat on the table in front of her, completely untouched. A waitress approached, unnoticed.

"Do you still want that?"

"Hmm?" Jessica murmured, brought out from her dazed state of mind by the sudden appearance of the waitress.

"Your coffee," the waitress said.

"Just another minute, please," replied Jessica.

The waitress walked away, and Jessica realized that the staff had mostly finished cleaning up. Some were leaning against the counter, idly waiting.

"Another day, another common coin," the waitress murmured as she approached her peers.

Feeling a little embarrassed, Jessica hastily took some money from her purse and left it on the table. She added a little extra to make a very healthy tip and quickly exited.

A man in a dank orange hooded sweatshirt and tattered jeans sat by the wall of the café. Jessica's street smarts began to kick in, and she walked slowly in the other direction.

A black mobile with dark windows drove up and slowed to match her walking speed. The window rolled down as a well-dressed businessman leaned out.

"Excuse me, miss, are you lost?" He spoke in a refined, cultured manner.

"No, thanks. I'm fine." She glanced over and smiled.

"I'd be remiss if I didn't offer you a lift. Where are you headed?" Such gestures were uncommon. Strangers weren't typically friendly, although vampires did occasionally seek out loners.

She gently pulled back her shawl to reveal the scar.

"Oh, Miss Winters, you enjoy your evening." He rolled up his window and drove away quickly.

The suit couldn't believe how close he had come, not just to losing his job, but also his head. It was widely known that Jessica Winters was "spoken for" now, all the more since she had been "marked", as the rumors went.

After walking a bit more, Jessica found herself in front of the parish church. The doors had been replaced by very modest fixer-uppers. To her surprise, the mounted wrought-iron lamps were still on.

As she entered the church, she found one or two attendees who were sitting and praying, trying to make sense of recent events that violently shattered their paradigms. Jessica looked up at Daniel's ceiling mural and then noticed a person leaving the confessional and rushed in.

"Father, forgive me. It has been weeks since my last confession."

She spoke so quietly that the man on the other side of the confessional divide could hardly hear her. He was a Nosferatu and was working hard to maintain the form of Father Frank.

"What is it, my child?" he replied.

"I am surrounded by the trappings that most people desire. But I am consumed by thoughts of the one thing that eludes me, one person who…" Jessica stopped short, unable to finish her thought.

"What is it that you really desire?" he inquired.

"I'm not even sure if it is so much that I desire him. I have always been so caught up in my career. I've never felt like this about anyone." She paused and sighed. "But ever since that first day I met him and I saw the world differently for a moment, life felt beautiful in ways it hasn't been for a long time. I'm rambling."

"Just take a breath and take your time."

Jessica continued. "I'm scared, Father. I could easily throw my life away on a wild chance. And in the end, he might just look at me as a symbol, marked with all of what is wrong with Anthrazit." She reached to the scar on her neck. "But if I don't take this chance, all that really matters to me could be slipping through my fingers."

"What does your heart tell you?" His prying for information was veiled in the cover of counseling.

"If I truly love something, I should let it go because if it's meant to be, it will return."

"Or fight tooth and nail for it. It's hard to know when to do which," he replied.

Jessica stood up and walked out. She paused on the stoop, pondering which path to take.

The Nosferatu placed his mini talkie in his ear and began speaking to Leonardo on the other end.

"She just left. I don't think she knows anything," he said as he relaxed for a moment, and his mangled appearance revealed itself. "How long do I have to keep this up? Impersonating a holy man isn't going to get me damned, is it?" the Nosferatu continued in an agitated manner.

"Just stay put; something has to turn up," came Leonardo's gruff response.

⊷⊰⊹⊱⊷

"Just a little further." Daniel's voice could be heard in the dark tunnel.

A light came on as he lit a small kerosene lamp. The space was getting smaller for the oversized gargoyle.

"We haven't been tracked, so I guess this long way through the underground has been worth it," his new friend said.

"These tunnels are massive, with passages that lead just about everywhere, and it can be easy to get lost down here. The vampires seem to hate coming down here for some reason too. This route is a bit of a detour, but there is something I have to show you first."

The dark tunnel gave way to the huge clearing in which Daniel had spent many hours rendering his mural. Daniel held the lamp toward the ceiling. Xi could stand with his knees half-bent.

"Wow. This is amazing. You did this?" He was astonished at Daniel's artistic ability.

"Can't begin to tell you the amount of time I've poured into this one," Daniel said.

"Days? Weeks? Oh, no..." Xi's realization was almost precognitive, but there was no time to evacuate. "Daniel, I wish you would have told me first."

Loud screeches were heard, and rapid footsteps approached from every tunnel exit.

"Your scent is all over this place," said Xi.

He placed Daniel behind him and grabbed the lamp, holding it to a dark corner of the ceiling. A creature with a deformed human frame crawled along the ceiling. It had leathery wings that webbed from its forearm to its side, grasshopper-like legs, and long fangs that hung down from its mouth. It screeched loudly at them. Then several more vampire bats swarmed from the tunnels and attacked with fury.

Teresa leaped into the air and snatched one with her powerful jaws. The gargoyle began to swing at them, finally catching one by a hind leg, and made it his tool to put down many others. Teresa defeated another as well.

Daniel saw an exit behind him and headed for it. Phoenix and her two mercenaries came running toward him from the far end, and he doubled back. Teresa jumped in front to protect Daniel.

After Xi finished off the vampires bats, he realized that they had been flanked and turned to see the new threat. He ran to the front and threw the vampire bat at the three. Phoenix made a slight shift to evade it. Xi used both fists to smash the ground, sending an earthquake-like ripple toward them.

As Phoenix leaped to the air toward Xi, he took another swing at her but missed. She was swift. Landing on his back, she crawled around a little in black-widow fashion. She made it up toward his neck, pulled out a blue glowing circular device, and slapped it on his forehead. It was a magic stone-powered muscle inhibitor. The gargoyle tried to move but couldn't. Soon he was rendered immobile and fell to his knees.

Teresa attempted to leap on a mercenary; he hit her with a taser weapon, and she fell unconscious to the ground. Daniel faced off with Phoenix, his back arched like a cat backed into a corner.

"C'mon, Daniel, let it out!" Xi mumbled, hardly able to form the words.

The other two mercenaries stood alert, but let their leader go for the prize kill. Daniel's eyes began to glow, and his upper and lower canine teeth grew. Phoenix charged him, knocking him to the ground, and sat on him. She grabbed his hands and pinned them above his head with one hand. Daniel squirmed vigorously but to no avail. With the other hand, she grabbed his face and looked rapidly from his left eye to his right, and back again.

"What's happening?" one of the figures asked.

"Just give me a minute," Phoenix replied.

She pulled another gadget from a back pocket. It was copper-plated, slim, and rectangular. A retractable screen shot up from the top of the device displaying written notes and an electronic drawing of a male figure.

"Did you see that? Looked like he was about to change into something," the male assassin said to his partner.

Phoenix pulled out one of her side arms and added a silencer barrel; she swiveled and shot both assassins in the forehead. She stood and removed the inhibitor from the gargoyle.

"You need to come with me...now! Rockhead, make yourself useful and grab the fur ball," she commanded.

Phoenix then used the same device to make a call.

"Yell-ow," the voice answered.

"I found him. We're on our way."

CHAPTER 15

WEAK HEIR

Teresa awoke slowly in a very unfamiliar environment with her senses dulled. She was in a humongous metal cylinder with one exit on the far side. She heard loud voices. But they weren't yelling at her.

"Get up!" a voice barked.

"Is that all you got? Come on!" they shouted.

She saw Daniel. Two guys were taunting him. They were well-toned fighters, conditioned in the fighting arts. Each held a long, wooden staff. Daniel was shirtless, and his scrawny frame begged for protection.

Daniel fumbled with his own staff, holding it more like a mop than a weapon. One of the men jabbed him in the ribs, and Daniel turned right into the setup; the second man gave him a hard thwack on the shoulder. He was slightly larger than the other, his complexion dark as mahogany.

Teresa leaped toward Daniel's attackers, but found herself yanked back almost immediately. They had chained her. She growled and lashed with one paw, her voice echoing in the large space.

"Wow, that one's got some fight in her," someone said.

A handful of spectators looked on, cheering and heckling from a catwalk above. Phoenix was among them, but she observed more quietly. A man came out from the catwalk exit and stood next to her. He was a bit shorter than she was. He wore a puffy, black, waist-length, sleeveless jacket, and an orange-hooded sweater. The hoodie covered his head and concealed his identity.

He joined Phoenix, leaning against the railing to watch the match. Daniel received a number of blows, and Teresa continued the loud protest. The man in the hoodie looked at Phoenix, then below. He placed his hands on the railing and catapulted himself over the edge, making the two-story drop and landing in the gladiator ring. The two warriors stood at attention.

"Take a break. I could use a warm-up," he commanded.

They stood at ease and handed him their staffs before jogging to the exit. The man turned to face Daniel.

"I know you," said Daniel.

"No, you don't," he replied.

"The party at the Hawthorne house. You were the bandleader."

He gave a smirk, the small, bulgy pockets on his mask showing signs of disintegration.

"My apologies." His tone was gentle, but Teresa didn't trust it. "Those guys don't really play fair, and they are so big. I mean, it's just not right. Throw away that broom handle. Just toss it to the side."

Daniel chucked the thin wooden staff to a corner.

"There you go," said the strange man, congratulating him. "You need a real weapon. Here," he said, gently lobbing one of the staffs to Daniel.

The nervous young man mishandled the staff, and dropped it to the floor with loud clanging.

Laughter erupted from the catwalk. The crowd had grown. The man shot a glance at them, and that was all it took for them to become as quiet as mice.

Daniel picked up the staff to realize that it was not that much different from the one he had previously held.

"You ready?" the man asked.

Daniel nodded and took an awkward stance, while the man turned away to take off his jacket and hoodie. Then he reached to the base of his neck and began to rip at it. His disguise was a mixture of a melted and molded leaf compound. Daniel was speechless. His new opponent had the shape of a man, but was not a man at all. He was built of a complex interweaving of roots, branches, and twigs. His dreadlocks were made of vines. He then focused on Daniel with slender, almond-shaped eyes.

"Okay, let's go," he prompted gently.

Daniel tried to overcome his jitters by making the first strike. His wild swing missed, and he was punished with a combination of blows. Daniel swung again and took a series of shots to the midsection, capped by a vicious blow to the face that sent him sprawling to the ground.

Teresa growled and stretched out the chain, but could not reach him. The audience reacted with an audible gasp.

There was a loud crash from the exit, and Xi appeared, yelling as he entered. "Stop, stop! What are you trying to do, kill the boy?"

"Are you sure he's the one?" the creature asked, looking up and addressing Phoenix. She bowed her head in shame. "Pathetic," he said, throwing the staff down next to Daniel.

He stalked past the gargoyle, barely acknowledging him, and Xi went over to help Daniel sit up.

The stone warrior had begun to wonder at the wisdom of his quick agreement to entertain the wishes of these tunnel dwellers. At first, they seemed to be on the same page, as they'd agreed that Daniel was a special child. But it quickly became apparent that they desired both him and Daniel join them in a standoff against the vampires. Xi kept quiet, as his greater priority was to get Daniel out of the city and in search of his true home. Well, maybe this last disappointment would get them out of there even sooner.

A set of keys landed next to them. "He is never going to learn if you pamper him," Phoenix said, approaching Xi from behind.

"You call this training? We have barely been here a daylight's passing, and all your people have done is beat the boy to a bloody pulp."

Daniel got to his feet and used the keys to unlock Teresa's chain.

"That's just it. We don't need a boy. We need warriors," she replied.

The tree man walked up and embraced Phoenix from behind. "Hey, Grass Mon," she said, nuzzling her face against the rough tree bark of his face.

"Sorry I was so tough on you before, love," he spoke softly.

Phoenix turned, and the two shared a passionate kiss.

"How can this be?" Xi exclaimed.

"Well, since I have no blood to tempt her..." Grass Mon shrugged.

"But the Root Clan eats people!" Xi blurted out.

"What do you know of our customs?" Grass Mon replied.

Daniel was in shock.

"That is only during the feast, okay," Grass Mon responded defensively. "Besides, she's not exactly a person, and we don't like the taste of rotted meat."

"Hey!" Phoenix objected, trying vainly to pull away from Grass Mon's embrace.

Grass Mon peered at Xi. "Root Clan, huh? I haven't heard someone use that phrase in a long time. Where did you say you're from?"

"If I knew you were one of them, I would not have agreed to come here," said Xi, sniffing with disdain.

"It's not his kin you have to worry about; it's my family," Phoenix said. "But why don't we just forget it? Just go. You can leave tonight."

Phoenix waved her hand dismissively. At that moment, Grass Mon noticed the fresh layer of bandages on her forearm.

"Let me see your wrist," he said, turning to Phoenix.

"Sweetie, stop being such a control freak," she responded, but her smoke and mirrors didn't work on him. He grabbed her by the wrist.

"I noticed you were itching at the bandages since you got back," Grass Mon said, as he began to unwrap them. "And you are always on me about recruiting more able bodies to fight—now you want him to leave? You are not being yourself." He revealed fresh gashes on her wrist. "Something has triggered your thirst," Grass Mon concluded.

Her bottom lip began to quiver. "That poor girl," she said. She could barely squeeze the words past the lump in her throat.

He embraced her, almost swallowing her in his arms. "Hon, you can't keep doing this to yourself. Come, we should still have reserves from Grace General."

Grass Mon kept his arms wrapped around her waist as he walked her toward the door. He paused and turned to Daniel and Xi.

"Stay a few days. We will help you teach him a thing or two. He might not be a warrior, much less a king, but every boy should know how to defend himself. Besides, we could use a new punching bag."

Later, Xi and Daniel sat in the medical supply closet.

"Hold still," the gargoyle said as he attempted to treat Daniel's swollen face with an alcohol-soaked cotton ball. "This was a mistake. I never should have agreed to come here."

"Was my father a good fighter?"

Xi paused. "This isn't about being like your father, Daniel. You will rule one day, and never doubt that you are destined to be a king. But maybe this is all too soon. And they are pushing too hard. The Root Clan had amazingly skilled fighters; we only kept them at bay because we had the brute force of the gargoyle armies."

Daniel kept his gaze fixed on Xi. "You never tell me anything about my parents," he said softly.

Xi nodded, and took a deep breath. "Your father was an incredible fighter. He had been trained in the fighting arts, long and short staff, and the blade, of course.

But the best was when he took form. His roar was so powerful it made both friend and foe tremble."

"I can't wait to go there, to see the kingdom for my-self," Daniel replied.

"You mentioned there is a desert to the north?" Xi asked.

"Yes, it is very big. I don't think anyone has ever gone too far into it."

"Well, then I think we should head in that direction. I do remember crossing a barren, dusty wasteland." The gargoyle mused over the faded details. Then he spotted Phoenix passing down the hallway. "Wait here," he said.

"Grass Mon is right; he needs to be trained," she said before he could even form the words he wanted to say.

Xi frowned. "Not like this. After a day or two, we're leaving."

"How long will you both last?"

"I was captain of the royal guard. I'll train him myself."

"Oh, really?"

"Yes. I might not be as fast as I used to be, but this form has its benefits. I'm starting to think—"

"Don't hurt yourself."

"Maybe this is all a power grab. You probably want to weaken your family's hold on the city to swoop in and grab it for yourself and your misfit ruffians."

Just then, Grass Mon's generals, a few humans, and two tree creatures rounded the corner.

"Me and the boys are going out to grab a bite," said one of the creatures, addressing Phoenix.

"Is eating all you guys think about?" she rebuked.

"There's nothing here to eat. Well, except—"

"Don't even think about it!" Xi stated forcefully. "That goes for both the lion and the boy."

CHAPTER 16
UNBELIEF

Grass Mon's room was surprisingly sparse—a three-hundred-square-foot space with a sliding-door closet on the left wall. Save for a bamboo mat and a rickety futon, there was not a single object in sight. The floor and walls were composed of solid concrete. The metal door was closed, but one could still hear the muted noise of the crew during the dinner hour.

Mounted on the far wall across from the door was a pair of swords in a crossed arrangement and an orchid plant in a tall glass pot, sitting on a narrow shelf just below the pair of swords. The orchid bore a large white flower, and the glass pot allowed one to see the beautiful, rich soil in which the plant was rooted.

Suddenly, the metal door flew open, clanging against the sidewall. Grass Mon and Phoenix stumbled into the room. He was on the receiving end of a heated flurry of kisses from his extremely passionate mate. He backpedaled into the room as she opened her eyes for just a moment to get her bearings. Then she stiffened up, looking around at the barren room. She turned and slapped Grass Mon.

He stuck his tongue along the inside of his mouth, testing the area that had received the blow, and then sat down on the sofa and hung his head.

"Where's the coffee table?" she barked, placing her right hand on her forehead and her left hand on her hip. There was no response. "And where's the floor lamp? You know how hard it is for me to find a lamp that I can sit next to without burning my skin."

"You are such a messy person. I had to clean up. It was like the stuff was starting to speak to me," he joked. Phoenix gave him a stern look. "Okay, I'll find you another one. Dumpster diving was the best part for me anyway," Grass Mon said.

"We made memories around those things. Plans for a future life together." She glared at him. "You weren't planning on coming back, were you?" she asked sternly, already knowing the answer.

Grass Mon stood up and walked over to the swords, running his finger along the blades.

"I should have killed Leonardo that night." Grass Mon's response was delayed, yet sharp.

Phoenix closed the door and walked to the futon.

"He was right there. I should have killed him. I will kill him."

"My brother is an idiot. I can bet he won't last five years as governor, and he'll do something to piss off the Family in much sooner time than that. Let them deal with him," she replied.

"So you would hate me for ending his life?" Grass Mon said, still looking at the swords.

"I don't know. Why take the chance of having that stand between us?" Phoenix answered.

He turned and locked eyes with her. "Sometimes I worry that you won't be able to make a clean break from your family. How do I know when you are with them, attending drink ceremonies and running whatever assignments they give you, that you aren't really enjoying it and would chose that life instead of being with us? Instead of being with me?"

"That's not fair—I don't enjoy it at all. And what is the point of me spying on my own family, if you are going to clean out and head into some suicide mission?"

Grass Mon sat next to her and wrapped his arm around her.

"How did you even make it out of there alive?"

"Well, that part is kind of hard to explain," he replied.

"Try me." She pulled away and looked at him.

"They took me out through the kitchen and out back by the Dumpster. A drone grabbed a meat clever on the way out. It took about three or four of them, but they were able to hold me down, and this drone started hacking away at me." He paused and began to massage his wrist. "Then the strangest thing happened. This short, old, homeless woman came walking down the street. She was wearing the oddest trench coat—covered in stars. It was dark, but I could see her, hunched over and pushing a rickety cart. The drone was soaked in my life sap, and he looked at the frail old lady as she scooted passed. She stopped and looked at the drone; the others looked at her and then at each other. I'm lying there just bleeding out, barely conscious. Then the homeless lady reaches into a brown paper bag in her cart and pulls out an apple."

"What?" asked Phoenix.

"She pulls out an apple, and offers it to the drone. 'Want an apple?' she asked. The drone said, 'No, thanks, I'm full.' He drops the cleaver and walks back inside—and the others just followed. When I looked back, she was gone."

Phoenix was not sure what to make of it. "Are you sure you weren't hallucinating?"

"Whatever. I guess it wasn't my time." Grass Mon shrugged. "So what are we going to do with this kid?"

"I think we should keep him here a few days. Really test him out just to make sure," suggested Phoenix.

"You actually believe he is some kind of beast warrior?" Grass Mon replied.

"Maybe I'm the only one that reads the text literally, but he has the physical features: mismatched eyes and the pointy ears. The legend says the great warrior will have these things and will overthrow all that oppose him. That wimpy kid is the only one I've found who matches most of the clues.

"Just hedging your bets," assumed Grass Mon. "Okay, sweetie. I'll do anything you want."

She looked at him and smiled broadly.

"When was your last meditation exercise?" he added.

"A while ago."

"Maybe you should do it more regularly," Grass Mon recommended.

She flashed him a look.

"Just to take the edge off and help you to refocus. You've been a little testy. Just sayin'."

"You think I should lock myself in a coffin?" Phoenix barked.

"I didn't say that. Resting your heart rate to induce a deep sleep to the point of death goes a bit beyond meditation, don't you think? And I'm not about to advocate anything the elders in your family endorse," Grass Mon said with a wink.

Phoenix relaxed, and he grabbed her hand.

"Come kneel with me on the mat. I'll show you something my parents showed me—it helps me to even out a bit."

They sat facing each other, with legs crossed. Phoenix looked at Grass Mon impatiently.

"Close your eyes," he said.

Phoenix huffed and obeyed. After a few seconds, she twitched. "Now what?" she complained.

"Now we just sit," he responded without opening his eyes.

She closed her eyes again, shifting her weight, trying her best to sit still. She brushed the edges of her cloak to the side and rested her hands on her knees.

A few moments passed, and then the orchid plant began to grow. The stem elongated and stretched like a vine, until the single tendril hovered just above the ground. The flower turned like a head, nodded in acknowledgment to Grass Mon, and then continued past him, approaching Phoenix from the left side. It encircled her, and Phoenix raised her eyebrows, sensing the slight disturbance. The plant froze as Phoenix reached in to scratch an itch along her ribcage. Then, as her hand retreated, the plant used tiny vines to snatch her personal device. The orchid vine recoiled swiftly along its path and back to Grass Mon.

Still with his eyes closed, Grass Mon raised his hand and caught the device. He squinted one eye as he switched it on and began looking over the images that Phoenix had stored on the handheld piece. He soon came to a large central icon without a label, and opened it to discover a curious collection of text. It was larger than any of the other files, with several pages and a few images. The title of the collection was, "We Are All Vampires: Teachings on Restoring Your Humanity." Grass Mon scanned through the stream of passages.

To be a vampire is not merely to be one that drinks the blood of a living thing; it is far more subtle. It is possible to have a thirst for blood and not "be" a vampire. We become vampires not simply because we bite others, but because we desire to possess and consume the life of others, and to use others for our own selfish gain.
—Fallen Saint

To be a vampire is to be a fallen being, one that has forgotten its humanity. What I say is difficult, but to enact real change, one must accept that vampirism is best defined as the opposite of being humane.
—I Believe

The lips are among the most sensitive parts of the body. They are filled with countless nerve endings, able to detect, respond to, and enjoy thousands of sensations. These fangs block us from being able to experience anything other than a hyper overgrowth of greed, lust, and anger.
—Sucker No More

When one crosses over, the constant pressure from this overgrowth above everything else drives us to blindly commit unspeakable acts of cruelty. Do not be tempted by the glamour and appearance of pleasure on the faces of your fellow turned or true blood siblings. This life is one that is truly cursed.
—Black as Crimson

*Blood is the source of life. To let your blood flow on be-
half of another is the ultimate expression of love through
self-sacrifice. To become a vampire is to be truly dead,
without blood and without life—without being able to
express love. Until the curse is lifted, we must seek to
give life and not take it.*
—True Blood Believer

*If vampirism is a curse, as we believe it to be, we will
need something incredibly powerful to break its spell.
This cure would be supernatural, something that bor-
ders on the magical.*
—Cold One 74

*There is a legend of such a magic: a young warrior
from an undiscovered country, with eyes that are un-
matched. The warrior is a powerful creature, yet he is
at one with his humanity. His ears pique to hear the
cries of the weak. At the sound of his voice, the world
pivots, and in his presence the most terrible of curses are
broken. If the existence of such a fantasy were real, it
would change everything. Consider your life a journey,
and perhaps he will find you. And if you should meet
this warrior, do as he says to find redemption.*
—Worse than Death

*Becoming human once again is a journey of redemption
that cannot be done alone; it requires the truest form of
companionship and friendship. How far along are you*

on your journey to humanity? Forgiveness is the true test. Could you receive a rival as you would a brother or sister? Could you love an enemy as you would a lifelong companion? Those answers are a portal into the land of your lost soul.
—Seeker 99

Redemption from a life of consuming others isn't a nice hope or wish of fantasy; it is vital. I might have no choice but to die this way, but it would be so much better if I didn't.
—I Was Hope

"You were right," Phoenix said.

Grass Mon was pulled back into the present. Her eyes were still closed.

"This feels good. I really should set time apart to refocus every so often." She smiled, and the sight of it was beautiful.

Grass Mon turned off the device and opened his eyes fully.

CHAPTER 17
BREAKING POINT

As a vegetarian, Daniel was prone to the midnight munchies. His stomach cramps were unbearable that night, and he staggered about the underground lair, prowling for a bite. "There has got to be something to eat down here," he thought. He had heard the loud ruckus as Grass Mon and his crew partied and feasted into the late hours, and he hoped to find some leftovers.

Finally, he came upon the room where the grand party must have occurred. His nose helped a little. Scraps of meat and leftovers were still scattered all over the banquet table.

Daniel spotted an apple and headed toward it. Finally, something he could eat! Then he saw a figure sitting in the dark, its boot-fitted leg resting on the table. It was Grass Mon reclining in a metal chair. He purposefully shifted the chair back, producing a loud screech. Grass Mon held a rather large drumstick, with pieces of roasted meat still clinging to the bone. "That has to be the size of a batting stick," Daniel thought. He gulped, hoping that the origin had not been human.

Grass Mon took a slow bite, ripping the flesh and skin from the bone, even as he glared predatorily at Daniel. He grabbed the apple and threw it at him. The fruit hit Daniel square in the chest, and he caught it on the rebound.

"What are you, exactly? Are you a man or a tree? Where are you and your kind from?" Daniel asked.

He was curious by nature, and the questions were not accusatory. Rather, he sounded like a naïve child.

"That's a story for another day. The question is not where am I from, but, rather, where are you going? And if you have the strength to make it there." Grass Mon used a fingernail to pick at food particles stuck between his sharp, wooden teeth.

"I'm not as weak as you think," Daniel stated.

"I don't think. I know."

Daniel stared at the table, and his nose twitched.

"Tell me, Daniel. Have you ever had to really fight for survival? Like your life depended on it?"

"Yes."

"I'm not seeing it."

"I spent two weeks—two weeks—sleeping on the street and in tunnels, working toward a dream that was destroyed in one night. I can take anything you can dish out."

Grass Mon did not respond right away, but he looked at Daniel for all of five seconds. "Believe me, you have no idea what I can dish out."

He flung the drumstick bone at Daniel, who ducked. It hit the wall behind him, and flesh burst in every direction. Grass Mon laughed maniacally.

The next day, Daniel showed up at the tanker stage earlier than usual. He had found a piece of twine and used it to tie his hair back in a short ponytail, proudly baring his odd ears. Grass Mon arrived and remained true to his word. The session was brutal, and so were the others over the following days. But Daniel became more defiant with each defeat, less willing to yield.

In between sessions, he would sit down with Xi and ask questions about his past. Daniel began to have a growing sense that Xi wasn't telling the whole story. So he began to pry.

"It seems you know about Grass Mon and his kind."

"Just what they are capable of," the gargoyle replied in a curt manner, and then sensing Daniel's unease, he added a few more details. "They are excellent fighters, and his companionship with that cursed woman is surprising. I'm glad they are willing to give us a place to hide out for a while, but I'll feel even better when we leave them behind. Let's hang in there and not give them reason to turn against us. Especially Grass Mon. Soon, it will be back to you and me. No more of these aggressive training tactics—I will take care of you."

Xi's voice was reassuring in just the way Daniel needed. He relaxed into the comfort of the statue's protection.

There were long stretches when Grass Mon, Phoenix, and the group's top fighters were absent from the hideout. Daniel could only guess that they were up to their anti-vampire activities.

On the evening before Daniel's scheduled departure, Grass Mon staged another gathering. He sat in a chair with his eyes fixed on Daniel, even as his peers partied recklessly around.

Grass Mon stroked his chin. "One more round? This one is for the road," he announced.

Daniel hesitated, but with a gulp, he decided to play along.

"Let's up the stakes, shall we?" said Grass Mon, and motioned to one of his men, who handed him a pair of large-bladed swords.

The gallery audience cheered and clapped. Xi approached the hesitant Daniel.

"This is what I was afraid of," Xi whispered. "Their kind can be a bit sadistic. Just humor him. If it gets out of hand, I'll jump in."

"Run away, run away!" someone heckled.

Daniel had learned not to be distracted by peripheral distractions, however. When Grass Mon lunged at Daniel, he got the sword up just in time to block the aggressive opening attack. Their swords clashed; Daniel parried. With a half-spin, Grass Mon got behind Daniel, and was following through for a kill swipe at his back. But Daniel swung around in time to guard himself. Grass Mon responded with a combination of strikes, but Daniel was able to block them all. Finally, Grass Mon planted an unexpected foot right to Daniel's chest, and kicked hard.

Daniel dropped to the ground, and Grass Mon got on top of him, placed his hand around his throat, and applied pressure. Daniel's face became beet red, and Grass Mon threw his sword to the side.

"What do you feel? Is it fear? Is it anger?" he whispered.

Daniel could feel the creature's breath echoing in his eardrum.

"Embrace it. Own it. Control it. Turn it into to something that makes you stronger. After all my effort, I wanted you to learn this by now. But since you haven't, maybe we should have the annual feast a little early."

He bit Daniel on the ear, just enough to break the skin. Daniel panicked and screamed as tears came gushing down.

Grass Mon stood and started walking away. Daniel rose up and chased after him, giving him a push on the shoulder.

"Hey, that was completely uncalled for!" Daniel yelled.

"I wouldn't eat you anyway—you're kind of bitter," he responded boastfully.

Phoenix walked over to Grass Mon. "Was that completely necessary?" she said quietly. "You've proven your point."

He held her by the waist and spoke into her ear. "You may be right. Can't put my finger on it. There is something about this kid, but I can't break through the layers of insecurity. I got a taste of it just now. If you can get the stone guy to give me a few more days, you just might have your beast man after all."

Phoenix motioned to the gargoyle, who joined them in a three-person conference. After a suspenseful few minutes, Xi turned and spoke.

"Daniel, it looks like we might need to stay put for another day or two," he said. "Some of Grass Mon's people spotted Leonardo's men patrolling our route."

Daniel's face fell. How much longer could he take this torture from Grass Mon? Xi did not look directly at him, and Daniel found himself, for the first time, doubting his protector.

⚔️

Late that night, Daniel was wandering the halls again, except this time he wasn't looking for a snack. He found

Teresa sleeping on some blankets in a corner of the tanker.

"C'mon, Teresa. Let's go," he whispered.

The sleepy cat stood to her feet, but wouldn't follow.

"Come on!" he said with a loud whisper and hand motions. But Teresa shook her head. "You know this would be a lot easier if you came with me," Daniel insisted, but Teresa wouldn't budge. "Okay, fine."

With that, Daniel left.

Under the cover of night, Daniel made it to the surface and onto a rail mobile. As it chugged and rattled along, he sat by a window and looked down at the infrequent streetlights. Even though he had washed up, his clothes still reeked of the sewer, and his face looked like a badly bruised peach. But his luck was about to change.

There she was, walking alone. He couldn't believe it! He ran to the door of the mobile, keeping an eye on her and looking down the tracks to find the next stop.

The dining room of Grass Mon's lair was packed with many rising voices. The room held most of his fighting crew, Phoenix, and Grass Mon himself.

"He even left the kitty. The boy has totally flipped," remarked a general.

"Whose job was it to secure that exit anyway?" the other general exclaimed.

"Okay, everybody, just calm down," Phoenix yelled.

Grass Mon remained quiet and pensive and then calmly asked, "Gargoyle, where would he go?"

Xi looked in from the hallway. The crowd had left no room for the colossal stone creature.

"He was very close with the clergyman of the religious site. But I don't think he would go back there."

"Would he go to Jessica Winters? Please say no," Phoenix asked.

"He told you about her?" Xi asked.

"No, but my brother seems to think he is really stuck on her. And hates him for it."

"Daniel does care for her deeply. He talks about her all the time. Where we come from, that usually means his heart has selected her as his mate," Xi replied.

"If he goes to her, he is more stupid than I thought. I put my brother on a fool's errand to watch Jessica. He'll be walking into a death trap."

"Okay," Grass Mon said and rose to his feet. "Phoenix, stay here. Gargoyle, get the fur ball so we can track Daniel." He then pointed to a select group, including his two generals. "One, two, three, four, and five. Gear up." Each number represented a trained detail with set responsibilities for the emergency mission.

"I'm coming with you," Phoenix insisted.

"Hon, this kid might be worth saving, but I'm not sure if it's worth blowing your cover."

"Maybe you're right, but I can't stand this double life anymore. A face-off with Leonardo will happen one way or another—it might as well be on my terms."

━━┥┝━━

Daniel made it to the street, but had no idea where Jessica had gone. Suddenly, he was hit with a sensation he had experienced only once before. With just a sniff, he picked up her scent—the beautiful fragrance with a hint of a sad sweetness. He started running furiously. With the slightest lack of self-control, he would have run on all fours.

Jessica had just arrived in the grand lobby of her condo when she heard him yell, "Jessica!"

"Daniel? What are you doing here?" She turned to see the winded and sweaty boy.

"I'm leaving the district and Anthrazit. All of it. And I want you to come with me," Daniel announced.

The concierge was slightly nervous, but remembered his training. As discreetly as possible, he got on his talkie.

"Daniel, that's crazy. I have a job, a life, and responsibilities. I can't just throw that away to run off with you," Jessica replied.

"I have Teresa. She found me, and we are getting out of here and as far away as possible. She needs you."

"What? How is that possible?" Jessica replied.

"I...I need you."

"Go home, Daniel. Better yet, you…" She began to stumble on the words. "You should turn yourself in. The police have been looking to question you, and they're probably on the way right now." She glanced over to the concierge, and he nodded.

Daniel stopped. He realized just how frantic he sounded. He calmed himself. Then he began to walk toward her. She took only a half-step back and bent her head down.

"I'm sorry. I should have thought this through. And look at me. I look terrible."

"And you smell," Jessica added.

He stood squarely in front of her, and this time she was the one avoiding eye contact.

"I have been hanging out with this guy who has been beating me senseless in the name of physical training," said Daniel. He took another step toward her and continued. "But I think quite accidentally," he began and reached for her shawl.

She grabbed his hand defensively. He waited for her grip to relax.

"He has taught me much more about love."

He gently pulled away the shawl and leaned in to kiss her—right on her scar. Jessica melted. It would still take some time for this to make sense to her, but she realized now that her heart belonged to Daniel. She wrapped her arms tightly around his thin frame.

The concierge stepped out from behind the counter. "The authorities are on the way."

He barely completed the sentence before a bullet pierced his skull, and he fell to the ground with his eyes still open. Jessica stared—in shock. He was a good man, with a wife and two kids.

The ground began to shake, and Teresa scampered through the entry, followed by Grass Mon, his team, and Xi, the gargoyle, who was the source of the rumbling.

"It's a trap! Daniel, get down," Xi was yelling.

Many more shots rang out from the frustrated sniper, and Xi extended his stone wings to shield the crew.

⇒+⇐

"Oh, come on!" Leonardo reacted in deep frustration, and began to reload.

"I'll be taking that back now, brother," said Phoenix, as she snuck up from behind with a dagger drawn.

"I should have known." Leonardo stood up. "Priest will be really angry."

He tossed the rifle at her, but it was a distraction. She caught it and also a quick roundhouse kick to the ribs from Leonardo. She responded, and the two engaged in rapid hand-to-hand combat.

The fight extended to the edge of the station platform. Phoenix gained the upper hand and knocked Leonardo onto the tracks. The fight extended further past the platform and to a precarious area of the rails. Phoenix made a miscalculated step, and the area gave out from under her. She hung by her fingertips from the elevated tracks.

"Brother, you wouldn't kill your own flesh and blood, would you?" she asked, deflecting her nervousness.

Leonardo brought his foot down on Phoenix's fingers. His anger began to boil, and he stomped, fracturing her third knuckle with a loud pop. Phoenix winced in pain, and Leonardo grinded further with the heel of his boot.

"How dare you choose them over us? You ungrateful, no-good, little…" Leonardo stomped again, as hard as he could. Phoenix screamed. "This wouldn't hurt if you were feeding. Abstinence has made you weak and fragile. You have turned against us for the last time. Our covenant is never to take the life of a sibling. But you are a traitor, and you deserve to die."

Leonardo paused, realizing that she wasn't about to let go.

"I find it a little ironic. Who's the assassin now?" he asked and reached for a pistol from a back holster.

At the sight of it, Phoenix did let go and dropped four stories. She landed on her feet, but her knees buckled from the impact. Drops like that didn't affect vampires who feasted regularly, but whatever fracture she had would heal soon enough and was better than taking a chance with a close-range bullet. She kept running with a small limp. Leonardo fired several rounds, but she was fast, and he was a terrible shot.

"All units move in now. Take them," he screeched into his talkie.

A horde of vampires and their hunter dogs converged upon the lobby as the crew took their stance. Grass Mon took point, wielding his family's signature swords. Behind him stood a line of his men, and Xi took the center position.

Grass Mon charged, and was surprised to see Teresa at his side. Together, they attacked the enemy, claws bared. Grass Mon was in his element—he sliced through a number of attackers with skill and efficiency. Teresa fought with a hunter far bigger than she was, but used her opponent's size against it and brought the monster down with stealth and speed.

Xi glanced at Jessica, noticing her barrette for the first time. "Heavenly stars," he gasped.

"You're Daniel's girl?" Grass Mon yelled out at Jessica. "You owe me one dead governor, you know that?"

"Stay down; I won't leave you behind this time, I promise," Daniel said and shielded Jessica with his own body.

The outnumbered group still needed to devise an escape, and two of them already lay dead. After the hunter dog was finished with a third casualty, he made eye contact and charged for Daniel. Daniel realized they were in immediate danger and grabbed a pole nearby just in time to spear the beast, whose dead body fell heavily on them. He stood up and threw off the beast, just realizing that he himself had begun to change.

Grass Mon looked over at him, and the two seemed to acknowledge each other with a strange familiarity, unlike anything Daniel had ever experienced. His new form was not quite that of the muscular feline beast he took on during his first change. He had only a few features, and looked more like a famished, hairy, stray animal. But it was more to work with than his usual scrawny self.

He roared loudly. It was more of an attention getter than anything else. Everyone paused for a second, and all the attackers made a beeline for Daniel. Xi jumped in front and made short work of the new wave.

Phoenix managed to reach the attackers, who did not expect an attack from behind. She drew her pair of pistols, opened fire, and then leaped on the back of a hunter and hopped from one to the next, making a kill shot on each.

"You made it." Grass Mon stood, covered with slime and ash, holding blood-covered blades.

"Of course," she replied, catching her breath.

"Any idea how we are going to get out of this?" he asked.

"I should have an icon for that," she said and whipped out her gadget, tapping the screen. "Everybody get in close," she commanded.

The gadget burned hot and bright, and began to scorch Phoenix's hand. A portal opened up, and the group was teleported back to the tanker in the underground lair. The group was dizzy and bewildered, and some were badly hurt.

Phoenix stood and threw down the gadget, which had melted beyond recognition. She stomped on it to put out the sparks.

"I knew I should have bought the upgrade," she quipped.

"Status," Grass Mon said just before stumbling to his knees. Coughing and wounded, he used his swords to brace himself.

"Positions one, three, and five are lost, sir," reported the remaining general.

Grass Mon was dejected when he realized that one of the casualties was his leading general.

"Okay, Doctor, you better be worth it," Grass Mon said, stumbling to a corner, where he took a seat against the wall.

CHAPTER 18

LIKE HUMANS

The entire crew still lay in the tanker area, trying to gain their bearings. Jessica looked around the room at the motley group of humans, a few root-based life forms, and the large stone creature. She was fully amazed and terrified at the same time.

While others were tending to each other or their own injuries, the gargoyle would not take his eyes off Jessica. Their eyes met, but she averted hers, not wanting to reveal how afraid she was.

"You have exceptional taste in jewelry," Xi commented.

Daniel looked at him, considering it an odd statement.

"Where are you from?" Jessica asked Grass Mon.

"I'm not from anywhere. I grew up here in Anthrazit just like you," he answered. "But, frankly, I'm tired of the masks you Commoners wear."

"I understand. Believe me, I do," Jessica replied.

Daniel went to help her get to her feet. But she brushed him off, determined to stand on her own. The room became solemnly quiet.

"Just when I was starting to think there was something more to you. If that was all you got, Daniel, I don't know what to tell you," said Grass Mon, breaking the silence.

"When I started changing, I could feel a connection between us, Grass Mon. I can't explain it," Daniel replied.

Xi furrowed his brow; Daniel could even hear the grind of stone against stone as the gargoyle clenched his gravel teeth. Despite the noticeable reaction on his face, Xi kept his thoughts to himself.

"What, does that make us friends now?" Grass Mon responded in an annoyed voice. "You could have gotten us all killed."

"I didn't ask for you to follow me," Daniel replied. "But you did, thank you. I'm not sure why you did, though." Grass Mon didn't respond. "Did you know Dr. Bol? Is he one of you?" Daniel asked.

Grass Mon looked away, attempting to keep a tough exterior. Without a response, he got up and exited the tanker area.

"You don't want to go there," warned the general. "Mr. Bol was Grass Mon's father. He's dead. So are his mother and cousins, all killed during Leonardo's raids."

Grass Mon reentered the room and went up to Daniel, who stood to meet him face to face. Grass Mon's dismissive expression was replaced by a seething stare.

"You think just because you met my father, that gives you an in with me?" He stood nose to nose with Daniel. "You didn't know my father, and you sure as hell don't know me." He pushed Daniel, who simply placed his hands in the air.

"I need to set up a medical treatment area," said Jessica.

"There is a room down the corridor that should work," answered the general.

"If anyone needs medical attention, just stop in and see me. I might not be familiar with everyone's physiology, but I'll do my best," Jessica said. Grass Mon looked at her. "Just earning my keep," she continued and walked in the direction that was pointed out to her.

Daniel and Jessica sat alone in the dining room. Even to Daniel, the room seemed uncomfortably quiet. They sat next to each other at the long side of the table, just before the doorway. Daniel scooted a little closer to Jessica, and she slinked back. She rested her hands on the table, fiddling with her fingers. Daniel reached out his hand to take hers, and she quickly put the once-idle hands to work fixing her hair.

"It's okay; we can take it slow. What's your favorite color?" Daniel asked.

Jessica shook her head, still avoiding eye contact with him.

"I'm messing up here, I know." Daniel tried to laugh.

Teresa entered the room and nuzzled Jessica's leg.

"Hey, girl, you're holding up really well considering all that is happening," Jessica said to the lioness, stroking her back. Then she began to address Daniel. "I'm not sure we have that much in common. We clicked that one time, but maybe it was just a fluke."

"I'm still the same person you met that day."

"I don't think I can handle these kinds of circumstances, Daniel, and I don't think you can either."

"But I will get there, and you are the one I want right there with me. I feel like I've known you for years."

"Because you read my book?"

"Yes."

"I've had guys use that line so many times it has become kind of funny."

"I thought you'd be thrilled. You like guys, and you like animals, so—"

"Daniel, that is so ridiculous."

"Wouldn't I be someone worth being with, someone you could study? The research find of the century."

Teresa realized there wasn't much steady attention she would receive there and headed out the door.

"A companion is not something you study. I want to be with someone who I can just be with. I love my work, but I don't want to have to come home to it at the end of the day. And that's besides the fact that you haven't even been on your own for that long."

"Just because you have spent the last few years working yourself into the ground doesn't mean—" Daniel's

rebuttal was interrupted by Grass Mon abruptly entering the room.

"Okay, limp appetizer." Grass Mon grabbed Daniel
by the back of the collar. "Let a real man handle this."

He placed Daniel out of the room and closed the
door. Daniel was shocked and bewildered as he stood
in the narrow passage on the opposite side of the shut
metal door. He could hear only a few muffled sounds.

⚔

Grass Mon placed his hands on his belt, bracketing
a shiny belt buckle. "Okay, Doc, drop your pants!" he
yelled over his shoulder, making an extra effort to en-
sure that the words were audible to Daniel on the other
side of the door.

Jessica stood up and looked at Grass Mon, folding
her arms in front of her. The two stared off against each
other. Grass Mon was the first to break his gaze.

"This tough act might work with Daniel, but it doesn't
work on me," Jessica said.

"I gotta give it to the little guy. He does have really
good taste." Gras Mon licked his lips.

"What is with your hand?" replied Jessica disapprovingly as she saw his hand give a twitch.

It wasn't the first time. Grass Mon shook both hands
vigorously.

"What is it—numbness, tingling? Could be neuro-
logical."

"Neuro what?"

"Sit down," Jessica replied firmly.

Grass Mon paused, but then sat down as instructed and rested his elbows on the table.

"Stretch out your arms," Jessica added.

Grass Mon complied, resting his twisted-root, arm-shaped limbs on the table. They rested still for almost a minute, and then a small twitch manifested itself in his left wrist.

"You're very good at compensating," Jessica said.

"So you weren't scared when I entered the room, huh?"

"Nope." She began to examine the length of his back.

"Why is that, trust-fund baby?"

"Hold still," Jessica answered, peering into Grass Mon's ear canal.

He didn't have an outer ear; the ear canal was where one expects it to be, yet with significant differences. Jessica pulled out her keychain, which had a tiny flashlight attached. She placed her left hand on Grass Mon's head and held the light close to his ear with her right hand.

"That is amazing," she said in awe. She pulled up a chair to get a closer look. "There is nothing there."

"Funny, my grade-school teachers said the same thing."

Jessica didn't laugh. "They were right. Really, I can see straight through. Fascinating! I was sure you had some sort of inner-ear imbalance, but this changes everything." Jessica prodded the hole with her finger.

"Hey, hold it," Grass Mon protested. "That's worth at least two dinner dates."

Jessica smiled brightly.

"There's that spark. No wonder Leonardo couldn't wait to get his hands on you."

Jessica's smile faded as she seemed to raise her guarded exterior.

"I was there to kill him, you know," Grass Mon said quietly. "At the masquerade."

"Why did you hesitate?" Jessica asked wryly.

"He's my girl's brother." Grass Mon noticed the look of recognition on Jessica's face. "Yep, makes it kind of complicated. This area is really hard to find if you don't know where to look. We've got a week, tops. Then I just hope Leonardo is leading the search. And this time I won't fail."

"Leonardo would have turned me. Daniel, in his own awkward way, saved my life." She paused and began to get lost in her thoughts and mixed feelings for Daniel. "I suppose he is more of a maladroit than man or beast," she added with a nerdy giggle followed by a sigh.

"Anyway," said Grass Mon as he stood up and walked toward the door. "Luring Leonardo into a last stand will take all the able bodies that we have. I'll let it sneak out that everyone should stop in and see you. Just use fewer big words, and no more stupid questions like 'Where are you from?' It's so upper Central."

Grass Mon opened the door and walked out. Daniel was still standing there.

"Orange! My favorite color is orange," Daniel announced.

Grass Mon snickered at him and walked away. Jessica looked at Daniel with a partial smile, and closed the door.

CHAPTER 19

BEING AND DOING

"What are you looking at?" Phoenix demanded. The narrow tube was a tight squeeze for two, usually meant for quick passage to a larger duct just a few feet away. She looked at her watch, bit the edge from a chipping fingernail, and cracked her knuckles. But Grass Mon's last surviving general kept his eyes fixed on her without saying a word as they both sat together in the cramped space.

The general was an outwardly strong, mahogany-skinned warrior in his thirties and physically well built. He wore a short-sleeved white shirt, revealing a bandage wrapped around his muscular left shoulder. The bandage covered a large wound he had sustained during Jessica's rescue.

"It's not polite to stare," Phoenix mocked.

"My apologies. I meant no disrespect," he replied.

"I should tell Grass Mon. He'll have your head, Number Two," she threatened.

With that, he looked away. He then reached into his pockets and took out a pair of silver cufflinks. After looking at them in the palm of his hand, he closed his hand tightly, making a fist. The general placed the keepsake cufflinks into his pocket. Phoenix watched him from the corner of her eye as he clearly wasn't able to remain still. The general took another quick glance and then looked away. He rested the palm of his right hand against the ceiling of the tube and closed his eyes.

"You're curious, aren't you?" She got on her hands and knees and slinked toward him seductively. "As we narrowly escaped with our lives, perhaps you pondered your life as a mere Commoner outcast—a nobody." She grinned. "Maybe you have been curious for some time. I've seen that look in the eyes of several men."

She drew closer as he attempted to keep his attention on the ceiling. Phoenix sat in his lap, breathing on his neck as she continued to toy with him.

"What's it like to be one of us? What's it like to be with one of us?" she whispered, but he continued looking away with a nervous expression on his brow and a stiff upper lip.

After long moments of silence, Phoenix relented and retreated to her position. She rested her elbows on her knees and held her head in her hands, allowing her hair to flow forward to cover her face.

"The answer to your question is no," he said.

"What?" she replied, throwing her hair back.

"I do not wonder what it's like to be a vampire," he replied. "I think being Phoenix has little to do with being a vampire. More than half of what one considers a part of one's being is still just the act of doing and not truly being. I believe one's self goes much deeper."

Phoenix rolled her eyes.

"How long?" he asked quietly.

She looked him up and down.

"How long can you go without...drinking?" he pushed on with a drilling stare. Still, she gave no response. "I would imagine you would get really sick to the point of death."

"I don't care," she replied.

He went back to resting his hand on the ceiling and closed his eyes.

"You're doing it wrong," she said.

Phoenix scooted next to him and knelt on both knees; then she rested both hands on the ceiling. "Your position has to be completely stable."

He joined and mirrored her actions, grimacing as the position aggravated his shoulder wound. He concealed the discomfort quickly with a bright white smile.

"Make sure your palms are completely flat against the surface; you'll get a better vibration reading. Two hands give you more sound to work with. And remain still, so that you can read the depth of the waves with better accuracy."

"Thank you," he said. "If I'm reading this right, there are definitely people in the chamber above. A search party maybe."

"Damn," she said. "They are close."

"They might have a hunter dog or two if they made it so far already," he mused. "We should get word to the other watch groups."

"Follow me."

They exited into the open tunnel, where mounted to the wall was a large iron wheel. Phoenix grabbed one end and the general the other. The two began to turn the wheel, straining against the rusted, heavy metal. Phoenix was doing most of the work—there were a few advantages to being a vampire, after all. As the wheel completed one full clockwise turn, a circular metal hatch shot out from a concealed pocket, closing off the narrow tube. The hidden hydraulics that powered the action then opened a smaller passageway in the floor. Phoenix started down, and the general followed behind.

⊶≺⊢ ⊣≻⊶

Slam! The inspector turned just in time to see the vault-like door swing shut behind them.

"Don't just stand there, you idiots," he screamed as he ran to the portal.

His team of vampires and hunters waded through the sewage toward the door. But it was no use—even with all their strength, they could not budge it. They were sealed in.

"Look up there." He pointed at a grated area of the ceiling at least two stories above, from which flowed the only source of faint light. "There has to be a way to reach it. Find something, anything."

They all began to scramble in the murky waters, searching for ladders and handholds. One of the hunter dogs began to whimper. Soon, the other let out a series of frantic howls.

A large light switched on, momentarily blinding the group, and a small speaker in the wall began a rapid beeping. The group scrabbled at the walls, but was swept off their feet when a flood of raw sewage poured through the grate above. The refuse filled the room, submerging all the creatures within.

⚊⚔⚊

"Team four reporting, sir," the general announced, and saluted.

Phoenix remained in a relaxed pose, but quickly took charge of the debriefing.

"We detected a search party in upper chamber twenty. I sealed it, just to be sure they don't get through. It will take the rest a few more days to work around the seal, but if they have more search parties in that corridor, we've got five days, tops," she said.

Grass Mon nodded. The general bowed and began walking away.

"She didn't try to get her teeth into you, did she?" Grass Mon yelled after him.

"Phoenix was her best self in every way, sir," he replied with another bow and continued on.

Grass Mon folded his arms. "Number Two is a poor fool," he said quietly to Phoenix. "When I found him years ago stumbling around in the sewers, I didn't think he would last a week. He's almost twice our age and will probably get himself killed. Number One had far more skill."

"He's all right," Phoenix replied as she watched the general in the distance, nursing his wounded shoulder.

CHAPTER 20
FOOD CHAIN

After returning from his scouting mission, the general sat down for a follow-up with Jessica to attend the large wound on his shoulder.

"What do they call you?" she asked as the muscular warrior took a seat on the stool in front of her.

He looked human, but judging by the company at large, Jessica had decided not to assume anything.

"Number Two. Grass Mon usually gives us a number, which can change based on our assignments."

Jessica gently removed the gauze from his shoulder. The stitches she had previously sewn were already beginning to break.

The general glanced over his shoulder to confirm that no one was passing by. "But my friends call me Na Mu." He added his signature smile.

They both heard footsteps at the doorway and looked to see Daniel standing with his hands in his pockets. Na Mu quickly stood up and stretched. "You know, Doc, I think I should just let it breathe."

"What? No—"

He walked away quickly, tapping Daniel on the shoulder, and Jessica tried to shout him back. "It needs a dressing!"

Na Mu lifted his other arm. "Later!"

Jessica shrugged and sat down, placing her hand on her forehead. "Daniel," she complained, "you drove an over-mobile right through the center of my life. Everything I worked for has been completely wrecked."

"I didn't exactly mean to," he replied apologetically.

"What *did* you mean to do?" she accused. "Better yet, what's your new plan?"

He stared at her, speechless.

"I worked all my life to study animals, not to run a triage in the middle of a rebellion. But I am doing what I can. These people, creatures, and what-have-you are all putting their necks on the line for you. Some have placed their dying hopes in you. What will you do for them?"

Daniel heard footsteps echoing down the corridor and spotted Phoenix just outside the door. She stood in the doorway, and Daniel nodded at Jessica before heading off in the opposite direction.

"Grass Mon said you wanted to see me," said Phoenix.

"Yes. Have a seat." Jessica gestured, taking off her latex gloves and exchanging them for a fresh pair. Phoenix, pouting, didn't budge. "Or stand." Jessica shrugged. "It's obvious you're sick."

"Needed a fancy degree to figure that out?"

"The vampire gene destroys healthy cells, replacing them with hemoglobin-starved, parasitic ones. Your abstinence practice means that the parasitic cells are having substantial negative effects. I'd like to find out if it can be treated."

"You might hold me over for a day or two," Phoenix said and smiled, baring her fangs.

"And what would you do on day three?" Jessica asked fearlessly.

Phoenix sat as she continued to grumble under her breath. Jessica began to unwrap her bandages, but Phoenix grabbed her hand.

"Grass Mon mentioned you would be sensitive about me seeing your scars," Jessica said comfortingly. "But it is the best place to start."

As she unraveled the bandages, Jessica gasped at the initial sight of the scarring that tracked up and down Phoenix's arm. The wounds were numerous and layered. Some were deep, others were shallow, and many of them were too recent for Phoenix to be willing to admit. Jessica choked back a sudden rush of tears.

Phoenix returned a dead stare. She then turned her head away and brushed her hair over her ear out of habit, unintentionally revealing a surgical scar on her ear. Jessica guessed the surgical stitching was performed a very long time ago. It had healed nicely. In fact, it was barely noticeable.

Phoenix turned to face Jessica abruptly and slammed her ceremonial cutting knife on the table.

———

Daniel sat on the catwalk, watching Xi perform drill exercises in the tanker below. He was drawing Xi in his sketchbook. Firsthand observation of abnormal beings had greatly improved his artwork.

Out came Phoenix with a furrowed brow and stomping each step. She stopped, looked down at Daniel, and then snatched the book and ripped out the pages. She tossed them over the catwalk and stormed away without a word.

The drawings fell gently, like oversized snowflakes.

It was time to do something. They couldn't sit around idly forever. He retrieved a few pages and set off to find Grass Mon.

He came to a secluded storage room in the section of tunnels they called home. The door was ajar, and he could hear hushed voices from inside. As he got closer, the voices became a little more coherent.

"Put it right there. Yep, that's good." The voice was Grass Mon's.

"Hey, Grass Mon?" Daniel pushed the door open, and his jaw dropped at what he saw. Grass Mon lunged and slammed the door shut.

"Okay, now you totally owe me," Daniel yelled.

The door slowly opened, and Grass Mon stood in the doorway wearing black leather pants. Na Mu and a couple of others were behind him, wearing similar garb.

"Come in and shut the door," Grass Mon conceded.

Daniel walked in with a showy stride.

"Knock it off, side dish," Grass Mon said. He picked up a crude hollow box wrapped with taut strings. Na Mu held a similar instrument. "It helps me think," he explained. "Grab that one over there. It was Number One's."

Daniel picked up the stringed object. "Grass Mon, we need to leave. Two or three days, and they will find us."

"Shhhh," Na Mu hushed Daniel loudly. "We don't talk business in here."

Grass Mon walked over to Daniel without making eye contact and showed him a couple of simple chords on the instrument. He then resorted to positioning Daniel's fingers on the instrument.

"Keep your fingers there. Now, with your other hand, just do like that. Got it?"

Daniel did as he was told. He looked at Grass Mon's hands to make sure he was doing it right, when he noticed the tremors.

"Don't try to get creative," Grass Mon added.

He walked back to the front of the band, turned to face the door, and counted down with his fingers in the air. On the zero count, everyone began to play except Daniel. He looked around. The band members barely touched their instruments, which seemed extraordinarily odd. The drummer's sticks didn't even hit the drums. The guitar strings were barely plucked. As for Grass Mon, he just pretended to wail into the microphone in front of him. Daniel could just barely hear the whisper of his voice. It was like watching a live rock concert in mute.

"Come on, Daniel, don't be a jerk. Are you going to play with us or not?" Grass Mon stopped the charade to chastise the stand-in. But the only thing Daniel could focus on was Grass Mon's trembling hand.

"Yeah, sure," Daniel muttered. He placed his fingers on the strings.

"Okay. One more time, from the top." Grass Mon turned his back and began his countdown. But just before he hit zero, Daniel reached over and pulled the huge lever. And a loud racket came from the large speakers.

Grass Mon jumped back, and then turned to give Daniel a scowling look. Daniel closed his eyes and kept playing his part, which sounded completely amateurish. What a loud, beautiful ruckus! Na Mu joined in, and so did the others. Soon, Grass Mon was the only one not playing. The band could hear many loud footsteps approaching; Jessica, Phoenix, the gargoyle, and several of their fellow underground dwellers rushed in to find the source of the commotion. Grass Mon started playing and rendering the vocals.

> *They say that if I loved you, I would let you go*
> *But I hope by now you know that's a lie.*
> *Fighting, clawing, biting my way back to you*
> *Please, baby, please return my love to me.*

Pretty soon they were really jamming. Their audience responded with a mixture of laughter and loud cheering.

"Not quite the sound of the old kingdom, but catchy," remarked Xi.

Phoenix stood, hands folded, trying to hold back a proud smile. Then she stepped up and sang with Grass Mon, making the song a duet.

"Nope, not the Central District Orchestra in the least." Jessica laughed as she couldn't help enjoying the spectacle.

Teresa resorted to lying flat on her stomach and using her paws to cover her ears.

By the end of the first song, the band was really hamming it up. They played a few sets, but the energetic performance died down eventually, and the crowd retired for the night.

Daniel, however, stayed up taking notes and creating diagrams in his sketchbook.

Grass Mon was walking past the small room where Daniel was seated. He took notice, hesitated, entered the room, and sat down. Daniel looked up, and Grass Mon returned a partially pleasant nod; Daniel returned to his note making. Grass Mon began tapping on the table.

"Well, that was fun, but I would guess we have just broadcasted our location," Grass Mon stated.

"Maybe it's time we stopped hiding," Daniel replied.

"We can't win this. The rebellion dies with us. It's my fault. All of it," Grass Mon said in a despondent manner.

After a long pause, he continued. "I was in school. Dad came up with a way to make a human mask from leaf paste. That stuff smells awful, but I wore it every day to cover my face. And I still couldn't fit in, even with the kids who would describe themselves as freaks. I tried everything: sports, a band, the whole nine yards. So then I met these guys, who said they wanted to change Anthrazit with a grassroots movement that would get rid of the bloodsuckers. What a joke! But I fell for it."

Grass Mon looked down at his hands and then glanced up quickly at Daniel, shame shining in his eyes.

"Let's just say Dad wasn't too keen on the idea, so he forbade me from hanging out with them. We started arguing all the time—'I didn't come all this way to raise a terrorist for a son,' he would say. But that didn't stop me. I couldn't stay away from them. Pretty soon, the vampires had caught on and started tracking us. I wanted to give them a place to hide until things cooled off."

"Those buildings at the edge of South Central—is that where your family used to live?" Daniel asked.

Grass Mon nodded. "I trusted them. I felt like the movement really got me in a way that my family never did. So I showed them my true face. Oh, they really freaked. One of them reported us to an officer. The vampires moved in so fast." Grass Mon's voice cracked. "I grabbed the family swords mounted on the wall, but I just couldn't stop them. It was too late." He leaned back in the chair and folded his arms. "I swore to avenge them. That night at the drink ceremony was the best shot I ever had. And I blew it."

Grass Mon placed his elbows on the table and cupped his mouth with his left hand. Eventually he lowered his hand and continued. "I'm glad we partied like that. Tomorrow, I'm ending this in one blaze of glory."

"A blaze of glory sounds good. But it doesn't have to be the end. I have an idea, but I'm going to need your help," said Daniel.

"What have you got in mind?"

Daniel cautiously slid his notes across the table to Grass Mon, whose eyes opened wide.

Jessica slept fitfully, twisting and uncomfortable. As she lay there, the door began to creep open slowly with a creaking noise. The stone gargoyle entered the room on his hands and knees. For a moment, he hovered over Jessica, casting a menacing shadow. His eyebrows furrowed—then he crawled to the desk, where she had placed her barrette.

He began to inspect it gently in his hand. He sighed, and his furrowed brow became a more sorrowful one. "Oh, great lord of all magic. I see the signs, and I know you are watching. Help me to be ready when the time comes, for I am surely not ready now. But I beg you to help me complete my penance and find favor in your sight."

Something made him glance over at the bed, and he found Jessica awake and staring. He gestured with a finger over his lips. "Please don't scream. I mean you no harm."

"Get out, or I *will* scream." Jessica's voice was low.

"See this? It's a sign." Xi proffered to Jessica her own barrette. "Providence is on our side. Whatever happens, we will see this through. I can't explain it—"

"You can't, or you won't?" Jessica interrupted.

"Daniel's trust and friendship mean everything to me," Xi said with his head hung low. "I believe your young love will be tested. Daniel will need you. Just don't walk away easily, that's all I ask."

Xi returned the barrette to its spot and left the room, closing the door behind him.

Jessica collapsed back and curled into a ball, shivering.

—◄— —►—

Early the next morning, everyone crammed into the tanker, all fifty of them, making a rough circle around the edges of the room. Daniel stood in the middle of the group and began to address the motley crew.

"Like many of you, I grew up in this commonwealth. For years, I struggled to fit in some way, somehow. It wasn't all bad, but now it has become quite clear; this is not my true home. I don't exactly know what I am or what to expect. But if my homeland is on the other side of the wilderness, I need to go and find it."

The group appeared stunned and murmured to one another.

"That's suicide!" someone shouted.

"Maybe—maybe not. That's why I am going with him," Grass Mon offered boldly.

Xi approached Daniel, who said to him, "Isn't this great news, Xi? He's going to join us on our quest!" Daniel spoke excitedly.

"Oh, Daniel, I wish you had asked me first," Xi replied with great hesitation.

"Na Mu, I want you to stay here, to lead anyone who doesn't want to leave. At the very least, our leaving will be a nice diversion to get you out of harm's way," Grass Mon continued.

"May I speak freely, sir?" Na Mu responded. Grass Mon nodded. "Even if you distract them, we cannot continue hiding in these tunnels forever. They know we are here, and they are searching for us now more than ever. There is nothing for any of us here. Permission to follow you, sir."

"Speak for yourself," said one man from the crowd. "I'd rather take my chances here, where we at least know what we're up against."

"Okay, fine. Whoever wants to stay can go with you, Number Six," Grass Mon conceded.

"I have a name. My name is John," the man protested.

"All who wish to stay, line up on the opposite side of the tank with John," said Grass Mon.

Bodies weaved as the sorting began. Low conversation could be heard as friends, family members, and lovers attempted to persuade each other one way or the other. Jessica slowly made her way to Daniel.

"Daniel," she said and then stopped, unable to complete her thoughts.

"I didn't mean for all this to happen. I'm sorry," Daniel stammered. "Maybe you can build a story about being kidnapped against your will, or something."

"You can't do this. It's too dangerous. You could die out there."

"Teresa will stay with you. Maybe you can get her to be more obedient," he suggested. "And if I make it, maybe I'll send her a playmate. A spotted white one, like you talked about in your book. Remember? They are out there. We just need to go far enough into the wilderness to find them."

The sorting was complete, and out of the total of fifty, less than half remained willing to follow Grass Mon and Daniel.

"Pack up, everybody. It's a road trip," announced Grass Mon.

Everyone began to scramble and make preparations. About twenty people had decided to come with them. Jessica went over to Xi and stared up at him, but the gargoyle wouldn't look her in the eye.

"If you know something, you have to speak up," Jessica commanded.

Xi frowned. "Daniel has to make this journey. It is meant to be. That is why I am here. If you decide to come with us, it will not be easy. That much I know."

The group moved swiftly and with some frenzy to load their essential gear into a number of mobiles and an over-mobile that sat in a large room several levels below the tanker. Grass Mon stood on the catwalk, surveying the activity. Phoenix came and stood next to him, wearing a worried expression.

"I hope you know what you're doing," she said.

"Leonardo's cleansing campaign killed my family. With just a couple of Root Clan members, these Anthrazit expatriates, and some exiles, we couldn't hope to do anything but die. But imagine we make it across the wilderness—how about that for a new adventure? Imagine we find a cure for you there. Isn't that a chance worth taking?"

"I'm damned. There is no cure for me," she muttered.

"We'll see about that. Don't worry. I packed up enough reserves for you, for the trip."

An eager teen root creature ran up to the pair. "Everything is ready, sir."

As Daniel lugged the last few heavy duffle bags toward the over-mobile, Teresa came running toward him. He knelt to greet her. The feline leaned against him and began licking his face.

"Hey, there, girl. What are you doing here? You and Jessica should have taken off by now." He looked up to see Jessica walking toward them, carrying a few bags of her own. She dropped the bags a few feet from Daniel.

"I guess it's my turn to make a choice, isn't it?" she asked as she stared into his eyes. "Okay, let's try and make this work. Let's see how far this goes."

Daniel embraced her, and they kissed. There were no fireworks, and his heart did not race. But for once, his mind was clear of the voices that provided both inspiration and anxiety. Finally, he had found a small, inner oasis of silence.

CHAPTER 21
GAUNTLET

Daniel sat silently in the trailer of the over-mobile as it made its way through a dark tunnel. He gripped Jessica's hand a little tighter to confirm that she was there, and she reciprocated. Xi sat meditatively nearby, with his legs folded and his hands resting on his knees. A group of humans moved closer to him, trusting him to protect them.

Daniel looked through a small opening to the driver's cab, where Na Mu had the wheel. The light at the end of the tunnel approached, and Na Mu kept his eyes on the path ahead. "Here we go, little man," he called back to Daniel.

Daniel pulled out his sketchbook and opened to where he had taped a map. He turned on a small pen-light to review the map, where he had traced in red a path that led through the Financial District and crossed the north of Central District into the Industrial District's main corridor and then ran on into the wilderness.

Phoenix stealthily pulled up beside the over-mobile, riding a liquid coal-powered, two-wheeled mobile. Very few had ever seen such a machine. It was fast and, agile, and it glided before the over-mobile with ease. Teresa ran along the opposite side, with Grass Mon on her back. Her exuberant joy brought a smile to Daniel's face.

"Okay, fur ball, let's stretch these legs of yours," said Grass Mon. Teresa kicked it into a higher gear until she was trailing Phoenix by just a few leaps. "Wow, you are fast!" Grass Mon exclaimed.

Phoenix shot out of the tunnel, and their expectations were confirmed. A barricade of patrol mobiles blocked the tunnel exit. The tunnel led into the main expressway that went down to the center of Anthrazit's Financial District. There were a number of pedestrian overpasses along the wide expressway.

It was the officers' third shift on high alert, which meant they weren't as attentive anymore. A few pedestrians paused on their way to their destinations, reacting to the fast-moving bi-mobile ridden by Phoenix. Soon there came an underground rumble that felt like an earthquake.

Phoenix flipped a switch on the handle of her mobile, and a pair of missiles appeared on either side. She pressed the button, and sleek missiles propelled forward. A couple of officers barely dodged to the side before their barricade was engulfed in flames.

Grass Mon emerged from the tunnel, picking up the pace to catch Phoenix. Na Mu and the caravan behind him sped up as well. The tunnel began to rumble as they raced out into full view.

Xi rose to a kneel, and Daniel looked through the small opening to the cab and through the front windshield. Phoenix's attempt had not cleared the road as anticipated. Xi clambered up to the roof of the mobile and followed it to the front hood. He looked through the windshield.

"Na Mu, keep going. Faster! Everybody else, get down and hold on."

As the gargoyle spoke, his large frame blocked Na Mu's view, but the general floored the accelerator. Large, dirty plumes of smoke bellowed out from the mobile as it picked up speed.

Teresa kept pace and moved to the left, while Phoenix maneuvered her vehicle to the right, allowing the over-mobile into the lead. The officers opened fire.

Xi used his body to cover the over-mobile and extended his stone wings to form a double-bladed battering ram. The over-mobile sliced through the burning barricade as the group barreled down the expressway like a riotous parade.

"What are you standing around for? Stop them," the lead inspector yelled.

At his command, the hunter dogs, officers, and patrol mobiles rushed down onto the wide street to pursue the group. Bat vampires followed in fluttering formation.

The officers opened fire again, destroying one of the rear mobiles. Xi returned to the spot that had been custom made to carry him at the back of the over-mobile. He shouted, "We are too spread out! We won't make it."

"We just need to make it to the drop, and we'll be fine," Daniel said, surveying his map.

A bat vampire was now above them. It swooped in ferociously, battering into the vehicle. A swarm of bat vampires were following fast. Xi ripped off the rear bumper and used it to smack the creature clear into the façade of a nearby building. He then waved to the back vehicles, coaxing them to pick up the pace. A few other bat vampires gained on them, and Xi used his new weapon to fend them off. But soon, another vehicle and its passengers were lost. Their numbers were now down to fifteen, by Daniel's estimation.

The pedestrians looked on, wanting to see how this would play out, but the anguish on their faces was evident. Most thought, "They will never make it, but at least for this brief moment, those rogues are free."

Suddenly, a young boy wearing a star-speckled shirt picked up a large trashcan and hurled it at their pursuers. Others joined in. A huge office copy machine plummeted from above, smashing the head of a hunter.

"Yes!" yelled Grass Mon.

A number of hunters now flanked both him and Phoenix. He drew one of his swords from a sheath strapped to his back and began jousting with them, all while attempting to keep up his speed. Phoenix pulled out her pistols and shot at the hunters, managing to bring down a few. But soon they were almost outnumbered, their run about to be cut short.

"Here comes the drop. Hold on!" yelled Na Mu.

Xi was almost thrown from the back of the over-mobile as Na Mu yanked the wheel and brought them down a sudden, steep descent. They were now in the drop—a large ramp that formed a steep decline into the heart of the Industrial District.

Many overpasses soared by overhead, and more commoners were lined up to pelt the vampire offensive. This was the Central District's gateway between the Financial and Industrial Districts. The buildings were taller there, and a number of them had large gargoyle statues on them.

"I never thought I'd see this area again. When I walked out that day, I swore I'd never come back," Na Mu commented.

The drop was starting to become a climb. A few members of the horde behind them were picked off by the bystanders, and two of the officers' mobiles spun out of control, crashing into each other. The horde was smaller, but not by much. And they were gaining.

Xi raised his head to look at the statues. "My brothers," he muttered.

"We're almost there," Daniel shouted to Na Mu, as he stood up.

"Daniel!" Jessica screamed.

"Don't worry. It's going to be okay," he replied. "Put me on your shoulders," Daniel ordered the gargoyle.

"Why?" Xi asked.

"Trust me."

Daniel reached out, and Xi grabbed his hand. A slight misstep left Daniel dangling dangerously, only held secure by Xi's grip. Daniel didn't panic, but held on tightly and made his way to the gargoyle's shoulders. Officers in the lead of the pursuit began to take aim.

"What is that fool doing?" Phoenix said. She looked up to see Daniel sitting on Xi's shoulders and yelling. The wind whipped his words from his lips so that she could hardly hear.

"Wake up! Hey, you guys, it's Da Il. Wake up!" His screechy voice was faint but audible.

For a moment, there was nothing. Then the gargoyles stirred, and ten jumped down from their precipices to join the fight. The regimen of ten stone giants engaged the officers, while Daniel and his friends sped away.

The newly resurrected gargoyles came in all shapes and sizes. Some were more creature-like and walked on all fours.

"Commander Xi-V..." He pronounced it "Tsee-iv." "They are leaving without us." A smaller gargoyle was addressing a larger one, who readily assumed a leadership role.

With a mighty roar, the leader charged the mixture of vampires and loyal officers. The other gargoyles followed closely behind.

"First contain the threat," Xi-V commanded.

They engaged their enemies, and the guns of the officers proved useless against stone. Drone vampires, on the other hand, proved to be a more even match in one-to-one combat.

An officer got on his talkie and called in reinforcements.

"Don't worry, youngling," another gargoyle shouted over the crowd. "If one of our brothers is with the prince, he will set up a checkpoint."

The bodies of drones began to pile up around the gargoyles until almost seventy vampires lay dead or mortally wounded. A crowd of Commoners had gathered along the elevated, rusting platforms of the dilapidated Industrial buildings. Some spectators used their tools, fists, and feet to fill the air with the noise of their rage.

"Magic is real!" yelled a woman from the crowd, and the noisy cheering boomed louder.

The young gargoyle turned to bask in the warm acceptance that he and his fellow infantry had received from the crowd. Suddenly, he was struck by a crimson bolt of lightning, and he began to crack and fall apart. The leader ran to his side and grabbed the rookie.

"MC-LL!" He pronounced it "Mikel-el." "Hang on, my brother." Xi-V spoke gently, but MC-LL crumbled into many pieces the more he tried to support him. The other creatures looked on in bewilderment, awaiting his instruction.

"That was a blast from the Royal Sphinx Ruby!" one exclaimed.

"Pull back!" yelled Xi-V, and the others followed him in retreat.

Another was struck from behind, and they hurried even faster in the tracks of Daniel's fleet. Despite their size, they moved rapidly. A few attempted to take flight, but could not. Despite having wings, their stone form had robbed them of flight.

The crimson bolt had come from the height of the sloping road, where a squadron of over-mobiles perched. The dark priest dropped from the skies just before the front bumper, and the vehicles pumped their brakes. Ten true blood siblings marched up behind Aitalas before Leonardo pushed his way through. He knocked into the priest, who stumbled forward. Aitalas turned and looked at him sternly.

"I thought they were all dead," a true blood brother remarked.

"Who?" asked Leonardo.

"That boy could awaken enough magic to destroy everything we have worked for," said the priest, not addressing Leonardo.

"Then we go after him," Leonardo said.

"But we dare not go into the wilderness. And who else would? We have made everyone terrified of it," answered another.

"Are those fangs in your mouth or an extra pair of tonsils?" Leonardo snapped.

Aitalas nodded gravely. "Tap your war chests, networks, and top performers. Give Leonardo whatever he asks. The three of you, come with me," he continued, pointing to three siblings. "Call your best assassins. Let's clean up this mess."

Daniel climbed down from the gargoyle's shoulders and made his way to the truck bed of the over-mobile.

Xi looked at him with amazement. "I didn't think you could do that," he said.

"You didn't think I could, or you didn't want me to know?" Daniel's eyes glowed, and he gritted his teeth as his fangs grew. "I could raise an entire army of stone gargoyles, crush the vampires, and take this region for myself," he concluded. He slowly relaxed, and his eyes became human once more. "But we will make this journey. I want to know where I'm from and what I truly am."

At these words, Xi looked away.

"Here we go," Na Mu said. He swerved the vehicle and busted through a guardrail, heading toward the red, arid horizon of the wilderness.

"Come on!" Grass Mon shouted, waving at Phoenix from Teresa's back.

"Are you crazy? Do you know how long it took me to build this thing?" she shouted.

"It won't last two seconds out there," Grass Mon yelled.

Phoenix stood on the moving bi-mobile and leaped onto Teresa's back behind Grass Mon. Then Teresa leaped over the barrier to join the back of the caravan.

The caravan stopped after they'd traveled only a few hundred yards. They waited, hoping that their new allies would join them before their pursuers got back on their track. Xi looked out expectantly.

"Just a little while longer," he said.

A dust cloud rose in the distance, and soon they could all see the unit of gargoyles soldiers who trekked their way toward Daniel's group. They hauled at a double-time pace, as their military conditioning was still mostly intact. Xi ran out to meet them. The leader and two others from the group ran ahead of their companions, and the four met and embraced as childhood friends.

"Brothers," Xi exclaimed. "Thanks to the gods and holy ones."

"Brother," leader Xi-V replied. Xi looked at the group. "I lost two of your brothers in the battle," the leader acknowledged sorrowfully.

They embraced again.

"I can't believe we survived the curse and that you managed to keep the prince safe," Xi-V continued.

"Xi-V," Xi greeted him by name. They grabbed each other's forearms, a traditional gargoyle greeting.

"Xi, you could have fed him a little better, though. He's half the size of my most-feeble apprentice," Xi-V said, attempting to lighten the mood.

"Xi-ii!" It was pronounced "Tsee Yay." Xi greeted him with the same forearm grab.

"How did he respond when you told him?" Xi-ii continued in a low voice so he couldn't be overheard beyond the group of gargoyles.

"I haven't. I can't even fully recall the details," Xi replied. "It is for the best, at least until I can figure out the missing pieces. Not a word, I beg you. I will tell him when the time is right."

"Well, you made it farther than we did. But how is it possible that we were in a populated region the whole time?" asked Xii.

Xi escorted his brothers to the caravan. Daniel walked out to look up at them. Some stood tall, while others were more hunched, but all of them towered over

Daniel. A few of Grass Mon's group walked up behind him, including Phoenix and Grass Mon.

"Glad you all could join us," Grass Mon announced his cautious welcome.

He noticed that some gargoyles, including Xi-V, stepped back to regard him and Phoenix with scornful looks.

"What is this abomination?" Xi-V declared.

"We should get moving. They won't hesitate to pursue us out here for long," said Phoenix.

"They? You mean your kind," Xi-V replied. "We will go wherever Da Il pleases, but not with the likes of you. Corrupted Root Clan, and damned souls. At Da Il's word, I would strike you down this very moment."

"Soldier, stand down!" Xi came face to face with his brother and exerted his rank.

Daniel found himself with an impossible choice.

"Your forces would make a small formidable army," Daniel replied. "These guys are beaten down, but they have sacrificed so much to join me on this journey. I am proud to call them my friends. Better yet, they are my pride. Right, Xi?"

"That's right, Daniel, just like in the old days as it was for your father, his mother, and all the generations before. The community of a pride—moreover a royal pride—is by the heir's choice, and its bond is stronger than all others," replied Xi.

Then he addressed his gargoyle brothers.

"Look at yourselves. Look at me. We are now nothing more than hardened dust. Despite this, we owe our allegiance to the kingdom; that hasn't changed."

Xi-V scoffed. "If the prince joins forces with their kind, the kingdom is as good as dead. The circle of gargoyle brotherhood is what truly binds us. Da Il must choose if he wishes to command the remainder of the gargoyle armies or rely on a savage, an abomination, and the rest of this riffraff."

"The name is Daniel," Daniel interrupted.

"I think it's time to go," Grass Mon said and pointed toward a distant dust cloud.

"Let's go, guys," Daniel said.

He turned and walked back to his group, with Xi reluctantly in step behind him.

"Wait!" Xi-ii ran over to join them, as did another of the gargoyles. The remaining statues held their ground and looked on in disdain.

"Okay, everybody, pack it in. We're moving out," Grass Mon commanded.

He sat in the back of the over-mobile with his arms wrapped tightly around Phoenix. The dry sun was sure to be harsher on the skin of a vampire than on the rest. Xi gave up his seat to Teresa and a few other Commoners. He was joined by the two additional gargoyles, and they ran at full steam just to keep up.

The pursuing vampires were in armored mobiles pulled by large, shielded hunters. The group of pursuers was led by Leonardo, who wore impressive plated armor. When they reached the remaining gargoyle army, they found that the creatures had become lifeless statues once more.

And beyond those statues wound the dusty trail of Daniel's weary refugees, wandering into the wilderness.

CHAPTER 22

VALLEY OF DEATH

"How did you know that would work?" Jessica asked. She cuddled with Daniel in the back-seat of the over-mobile. "How did you know they would awaken?"

"I didn't know for sure, but I get these strong inklings when I'm around Xi, Grass Mon, and Teresa. I had those about the statues too," Daniel replied, filled with disappointment.

Jessica put her head on his shoulder, and he took her hand and knotted it with his; she felt a nervous respect for this new side of Daniel. He gazed out into the haze. "I still can't believe they wouldn't join us. They hated Grass Mon right away; there's something there I need to get to the bottom of. Sometimes I get the sense that Xi is holding out on me."

Jessica wavered on whether to divulge her late-night encounter with Xi, who ran and breathed heavily just a half step behind the vehicles.

"I wonder how much longer Xi and his brothers can keep going before we will need to stop," she said.

"Sorry for wrecking your life," Daniel said.

Jessica looked at him without answering for some time. "It's okay. It was falling apart anyway," she finally replied. "My advisors were right; I never should have taken over the preserve. At first I thought I could use its resources to help continue exploration of the wilderness and the creatures out here. But things quickly started working in reverse."

"Are you sure this is the right way?" Na Mu asked loudly without taking his eyes off the road.

Daniel pulled out his large map and reviewed the course. Much of his annotations were guesswork once they crossed into the wilderness. Jessica leaned in to offer her knowledge, which would certainly be much better than traveling completely blind.

Dust now covered the ground and swirled in the air above them, even masking the typically smog-covered expanse.

"Keep going straight. Some rock formations should appear soon, and then bear right," Jessica instructed.

The over-mobile starting to bounce a bit as the ground of powdery sand revealed uneven rocks beneath. The oversized mobile carried about ten passengers and most of the supplies they hoped would help them make the trip. Light began to dim, and the sand-filled winds grew more intense. The best they could do was pray that the coal engines would hold up.

"At this pace we should make the Grand Rocks by nightfall, and then it's another day's journey to Winters Valley." Jessica had named it in memory of her parents. "After that, we'll have to put our trust in Teresa's instincts to lead us through whatever undiscovered lands lie beyond that point."

"How come you never went much farther?" Na Mu asked.

"The terrain leading out of the valley becomes much more treacherous, and it proved too risky. Making it to Winters Valley with such a big group has never even been attempted," she answered.

A dark void filled the sky by the time they checked in at Grand Rocks. The naturally sculpted rock formations made it an ideal place to camp. A large cave was suitable for many of the passengers, while others roughed it in tents at the cave's entrance. Xi and his brothers rotated a two-guard, one-rest watch schedule.

Grass Mon, Daniel, and a few others, including Na Mu and Phoenix, sat around a fire to strategize.

"Leonardo didn't pursue us right away. Instead, he reequipped with a non-coal transport of hunter-drawn vehicles. He's much smarter than I gave him credit for," said Phoenix. "Less fuel and weight. He'll be slower for now until our vehicles run out of coal."

"Why would he pursue us? You would think he'd just let us go. We are no longer in Anthrazit, and pose no threat to him," said Na Mu. "Do you ever get the feeling there's something you don't know that you don't know?" He glanced at Phoenix.

"Okay, so he's on non-coal transport. Let's use that to our advantage while we can," Grass Mon stated. "If we keep moving ahead on coal, my guess is that we can keep at least a day ahead. We'll have to abandon the mobiles once they run out of fuel."

"Maybe we can keep them going a bit farther if we can devise some sort of harness for the gargoyle brothers," Daniel offered.

"Good call, Daniel. Actually, let's do that before all the fuel is gone," Grass Mon replied.

"But won't that allow them to catch up sooner, sir?" Na Mu added.

"Yes, but we will not outrun them the whole way, so we might as well set the terms for when we engage them. Preserving some coal will give us an exit strategy," Grass Mon said. Then he smirked. "Look who's finally growing a backbone and contributing more. It's about time."

Phoenix stood up. "The front axles are busted on at least two of the mobiles. With some adjustments, we could get them to run on just one wheel in front. This should also help reduce our fuel-burn rate. You three, come with me," she said, pointing to a few people who stood on the outer part of the circle. She led them toward the parked mobiles as the circle dispersed.

Daniel returned to the cave, where he found Jessica working by the light of a dim candle in a jar. She had managed to meticulously catalogue new samples and lay them out next to her portable microscope.

"What time are you going to sleep?" she asked.

"Soon," Daniel replied.

He picked up his sketchbook and sat with his back against the cave wall. Jessica moved swiftly from her notes to the small glass beakers containing liquid samples. Referring to her notes one more time, she began to mix the contents of the two beakers. The new compound became solid as a rock, and then changed quickly to a liquid, caught fire, and exploded.

Jessica gasped, and Daniel ran to her side to make sure she was okay. "What happened? Are you all right?" he asked.

"I'm fine. I was almost sure I had it figured out," Jessica said to herself aloud.

"Could it be?" Daniel asked. "Am I in love with a mad scientist? I worried how all this would impact you, your love for science and certainty. All of this stuff—it's happening to me, so I have no choice but to see it through. But you could walk away anytime you want."

"Well, we're in the middle of the wilderness, so I'm stuck with you now," she mocked.

Jessica looked up, imagining her parents looking down on her. She then closed her eyes. "My dad used to say, 'The study of science to prove what you already know lacks imagination.' I'd like to think he would have been very proud of me today."

"Based on what you've told me about your dad and mom, I think they would be proud of you every day, no matter what," Daniel said as he continued to sketch.

Jessica smiled at hearing those words.

"It's nice to be able to draw you when I can look at you and not have to guess what your exact features are like."

"I look like a mess," she replied.

"You're perfect."

Phoenix came in at just that moment and snatched his sketchbook away. Daniel pursued her. "What is your problem?" he asked.

"The only reason you're still alive is that there's still some slim chance that, in saving you, I'll save myself. But I swear, the moment we learn otherwise, I will be the first one biting on your neck." She ripped the pages into tiny pieces and tossed them up in the air as she walked away.

"There's a lot more paper where that came from," Daniel taunted as she left.

Without turning around, she flipped him her middle finger as a parting gift. With a deep sigh, Daniel looked around for his fighting staff and walked over to retrieve it.

"Art is not your weakness, you know. It's your strength," said Jessica.

"I should practice my combat," replied Daniel as he walked out.

He stood by the campfire, and began practicing a series of moves against an imaginary opponent. Grass Mon reclined nearby, plucking out a new tune on his stringed musical instrument.

"You're fighting against the weight of the staff," Grass Mon announced.

He put down his instrument and walked toward Daniel, eventually standing in front of him to instruct him. "When you lunge, try to keep your forearm firm. Lock your elbow only after making contact."

He took Daniel's elbow and straightened his arm. Daniel kept staring at Grass Mon's jittery hands.

"It's something in my head," he explained. "Sometimes my limbs get the message of what I want them to do. Other times, they don't."

"I've noticed it's getting worse," Daniel replied.

"Yep. It's probably from this desert climate." Grass Mon walked over to his gear and picked up a sword. "Okay, follow me."

He led Daniel in a series of handling drills. They were soon joined by Na Mu and a few others. The group practiced by the fire late into the dark night.

At daylight's first break, Phoenix woke up yelping. Daniel had fallen asleep sitting on a rock and holding a sword. He awoke just in time to notice Phoenix in mild distress.

"Ah, damn it! What the hell?" Phoenix screamed. She hopped around and smacked her legs and hands, which had begun to smolder. The smoke rose from the surface of her skin, almost as if she had fallen into the campfire. Phoenix ran into the cave, searching for Jessica.

Daniel rose to his feet in a drowsy stupor and shook Grass Mon. "Come on, friend, let's get going."

Daniel was finally able to get him up. The camp packed up and prepared for the journey ahead.

Teresa was more in her element there in the wilderness, now thriving more than ever. After eating several pieces of stored meat, she was filled with energy and jogged along with the gargoyles, but Daniel could tell that she was eager to stretch her legs. He also noticed Jessica looking on in admiration of her from the back of the oversized mobile. He stood and waved to Teresa, who ran up next to the moving over-mobile.

Daniel reached down to Jessica. "Come on." She took his hand, but let go as soon as she realized what he was planning.

With a grin, Daniel leaped over the side of the moving vehicle and onto Teresa's back. The group onboard the over-mobile cheered, and Na Mu slowed down a little when he noticed what was happening.

"Come on," Daniel repeated.

Finally, Jessica climbed over the edge. She jumped on just behind Daniel, letting out a half-panicked yelp.

Teresa sprinted up to Na Mu's driver side. "We're going to scout ahead," Daniel announced.

"Go for it," Na Mu replied.

"Hang on tight, okay?" Daniel said to Jessica, who responded by placing her arms firmly around his thin waist.

With that, Teresa dashed ahead like a bolt of lightning as the group cheered loudly.

"Wow, can't keep that in a cage," said Na Mu as he watched them vanish into the distance.

After a long stretch, Teresa slowed the exhilarating ride. As Jessica still clutched on to Daniel, he could hear her heart, still racing with thumping beats through her chest and on his back. He turned to face her.

"I nearly lost my glasses," Jessica said as she smiled.

Daniel leaned in and kissed her, interrupting her effort to straighten her frame.

Teresa let out a low growl. Daniel could sense that his counterpart was worried. He looked forward, peering into the distance.

"It seems the further we get from Anthrazit, the stronger Teresa has become despite the harsher climate," Jessica commented.

"You're right, Teresa. That doesn't look good," Daniel muttered.

"What's wrong?" Jessica asked.

"Looks like a sandstorm is heading this way."

"You can spot that? All I can see is haze."

"What should we do? Should we camp?" he asked.

"There isn't much cover here. If what you're saying is true, we might have to push through it."

Jessica looked around at the soft, rolling sand. Nothing offered as much as a nook or cranny to shelter the travelers. The atmosphere thickened with strange, dark clouds that hovered above like tattered veils.

"Can't we just make it to Winters Valley and buckle down?"

"If we make it that far, we'll need to keep going. The valley intensifies the winds, and the wolf beasts track through there, hoping..." She caught herself thinking back to that fateful night. "Hoping that some creature will make that mistake."

"Okay, let's go warn the others," replied Daniel.

They raced back to join the group and began to describe the situation. There was a lot of resistance.

"That's crazy. We'll never make it," responded a vocal young woman among the travelers.

"We don't have any choice," Jessica responded.

"She's right." Xi backed Jessica. "Rest now, and Leonardo's forces will catch us unprepared and at a disadvantage."

"If we don't camp, that would force us to go two days straight without rest, and into a storm no less," said another voice of dissent.

"It's not ideal," Na Mu noted.

"Not ideal? Are you kidding me?" the man pressed the issue.

"We keep moving," Grass Mon insisted, putting his foot down.

The caravan shifted out of cruise control and prepared to take the storm head on. The violent swells of dusty winds became more intense with every moment. Before they knew it, they were swallowed up in the sandstorm. Soon, the forceful winds threatened to lift the vehicles from the ground. The sand drifts were knee deep.

Goggles were an occasional fashion statement in Anthrazit, or a prerequisite for the overly health conscious, but they became vital at this point, and were in short supply. The tiny particles of sand blasted their faces, into eyes, ears, and throats, rubbing every exposed area of skin like sandpaper.

"Oh, God, are we even halfway through?" someone yelled.

"Gray and Red, lead in front and shield us as much as you can," Daniel instructed the two new gargoyles. The group had assigned affectionate nicknames for Xi's gargoyle brothers based on the color of the stone that they had become.

As they spread their wings, forcing the winds around the vehicles, the move proved to be an effective shield against the storm. This also led to an amazing realization. The gargoyles were not impacted by the storm; Xi and his brothers seemed immune to it. They trudged along as towering warriors, immune to the winds and sand. Teresa was also less susceptible, though to a smaller degree.

They reached Winters Valley and decided to camp for several hours to allow the brunt of the storm to pass. As they waited, Jessica reflected on the humble memorial she had placed in honor of her parents. The memorial plaque was attached to a rock anchor deep in the ground next to the mobile her parents traveled in when she was a child.

Ready to push ahead, they decided to bank on the gargoyles' newfound strength. The group cut all the coal engines and harnessed Gray and Red to tow the over-mobile, which they packed with more supplies and passengers. Xi towed another large mobile, and Teresa pulled a smaller vehicle. They kept two mobiles going on coal, while two were completely abandoned at Winters Valley.

They surveyed the jagged cliffs rising to either side of the valley.

"That path appears to be the only way out." Grass Mon pointed toward the highest cliff and the treacherous, undeveloped path ahead.

They headed up by a thin trail. As anticipated, the storm intensified. It pushed upward at the entrance to the cliffs and punished them for daring to be so bold. Soon, save for the gargoyles, they couldn't see beyond an outstretched hand. Even with the help of the engines, everyone needed to contribute to towing and pushing the vehicles with ropes and whatever else they could find.

They were homeless pilgrims now caught in limbo; they had come too far to turn back and yet had no hope of making it to the other side of the storm. Suddenly, a huge burst of wind ripped a vehicle and its driver off the edge of the cliff. The group in front had harnessed themselves to it to protect themselves, but it only served as a device for the sandstorm to claim more victims.

A powerful funnel of winds formed halfway up the cliff. The winds picked up Gray and Red, almost claiming them as well, but they dug their claws in. Everyone tried to hold on. It seemed as if they were in a stalemate. Daniel and his friends wouldn't let go, and the storm wouldn't relent. But the storm had more to give. A large gust sent Gray and Red flying past the over-mobile. Their weight now worked against the vehicle and its crew, threatening to undo them all. The over-mobile made a complete 180-degree turn. Red and Gray clung to the edges of the cliff, and Teresa was occupied with her mobile. She clasped her jaws around the rear fender, pulling as hard as she could to secure it.

"Just hold on. We're coming," a voice whispered through the howling winds.

They looked up to see a large, silhouetted, animal-like creature. Then without a moment more to spare, two gigantic snow leopards emerged like mirages from the flying, sandy grit. Their white-spotted fur coats seemed untainted by the dirt that flew all around. The twin snow leopards were fully impervious to the storm. They were each almost double the size of Teresa, yet they moved with majesty and grace.

They grabbed the over-mobile in their powerful jaws, and with a couple of gentle tugs, the vehicle was on a more secure ledge. Without fear or question, a number of the group climbed on their furry backs and held on, as the pair of leopards continued to tow the mobile to safety. In a few moments, those who remained made it to the top. The sandstorm was now mostly below them. They marveled at the strange phenomenon.

At the peak awaited the beast-man that had given them just enough hope to hold out. He appeared to be like the snow leopards but walked on two legs and had many features like a man.

"You have returned." The creature spoke with a certain nobility, but also with excitement. He ran toward them, knocking Daniel aside. He crouched nose to nose with Jessica and wagged a small, bushy tail.

"Amazing," said Jessica. "Are you a beast or a man?"

"But, of course. Oops, it has been so long, I kind of forgot."

He stood back and began to transform. He was a fit older man with long, snow-white hair and a flowing beard. Some of his hair and beard had been bound in beaded locks, and he wore a finely crafted leather tunic. His pale-pink complexion showed a number of wounds, each of which seemed to have a story of its own. Jessica stared, stunned.

"It was you?" she replied, on the verge of tears.

He laughed boldly and scooped her up in a bear hug.

"My sign, my oracle," he replied. "I knew I would see you again."

CHAPTER 23
UPRISER

"Waii? Is that you?" Xi couldn't believe his eyes.
"Xi? No way! What happened to you?"

They ran toward each other and grabbed the other's opposite forearm. "You look horrible," Waii said and laughed heartily.

"You look so mature," said Xi.

A lump formed in his throat. Waking up to a well-developed town and now seeing Waii this much older, Xi was starting to put the pieces together.

"It's been a long time," remarked Waii.

"Believe me, you have no idea," Xi replied.

"Let's get you guys out of this mess," said Waii, looking over at the snow leopards. "Lassa...Bassa."

Without any further instruction, they took to the task of moving the heavy load, fully disciplined and compliant. The group began a short trek, surveying the marvelous view from the penultimate peak. They could see other peaks in the distance and cloud-covered desert areas below. Within a few moments, they came to a large cavern, with a stream running through the center.

It was a home fit for a desert king. The walls of the cavern were made of marbleized layers of rock, and the ripples of water from the stream cast a shimmering light against it. One area was cultivated into a luscious garden, with carefully organized vegetation, which produced appetizing fruits of an amazing variety.

The travelers quickly made themselves at home. Xi and the caravan's leaders sat in a large circle around a well-crafted, white-stone fire pit. Waii got a healthy fire going quickly. Xi used a long metal poker to jab at coals and stoke the flames.

"It was bad, everything just falling apart around me. I couldn't believe I made it out alive." Waii reflected on the past. He began to stare at Xi with a grave expression.

Xi was excited to reconnect with Waii, and for this touch of the homeland he once knew, but his mind was burdened with this anomaly. Waii locked gazes with him.

"You haven't aged at all. Neither have your brothers," said Waii. "I've seen strange things out here. I've seen storms that move sideways, mirages of the old kingdom appearing and vanishing. And now you, sitting here in front of me, made of stone and not a day older than the last days of the kingdom."

"Magic is at work, old friend. The father of magic is at work on a massive scale," Xi said pensively as he looked at Daniel. "We need to be faithful."

"We are sphinx," Waii replied softly.

"Waii, I present to you the rightly pledged heir to the throne, Da Il." With those words, Xi walked behind Daniel and placed his hands on the boy's shoulders.

Waii took two steps back and covered his mouth, trying to withhold the chuckles. Xi left Daniel's side and walked over to his old friend.

Waii leaned over to whisper in Xi's ear. "I'm not sure what prank you're pulling on this kid. The father of magic hates deception most of all."

Xi's eyes narrowed.

"I'll play along. I'm old and could use a really good laugh," Waii added.

"Waii was less than half your age when the kingdom fell. He hadn't even done his rite of passage," Xi said to Daniel, swelling with pride. "Now, he is living and thriving where nothing seems to be able to endure. And with two counterparts? Very unusual," Xi continued, adding emphasis to the number.

Waii gestured with three fingers. "The wolves are unrelenting and travel in large packs, but we hold our own."

Waii sat and began shelling some peanuts and eating them, tossing the shells into the fire.

"I've got a counterpart too," Daniel said, looking at Teresa with pride.

"Oh, do you?" Waii responded with a wink.

"She is so undisciplined," Xi said apologetically.

Waii looked into the flames. "So when did the Gargoyle Royal Guard start spending time with the Root Clan?" he asked, glancing condescendingly at Grass Mon, who was slumped against the wall of the cavern. Too exhausted to fight, he stood up and headed for the miniature stream.

"Grass Mon, wait," Jessica said, trailing along and leaving Daniel to once again choose sides.

Grass Mon knelt at the stream and closed his eyes meditatively. Teresa sat next to him as Jessica stroked her fur.

"I sense myself getting closer to my homeland. I can feel it deep inside. But it seems that scorn follows me wherever I go," said Grass Mon. He scooped handfuls of water and washed his face almost ceremonially, and the twigs, roots, and bark that made up the topography of his body drank it in.

"I think at some point we all stop caring. We do what we know is right. Whether ahead or behind, what others think of us really doesn't matter anymore," Jessica said, and stood, walking back to the old boys' club, where. Daniel was still trying to fit in.

"Why did you call me your oracle?" Jessica asked Waii boldly. Whatever their topic was before was not of interest to her.

"I was praying for a sign. Something that would say there is more to life than finishing out my days here. Something worth fighting for, I guess. Then there you were. I had to save you." He stood and boastfully walked over to Jessica, flexing his biceps. "So tell me, oh, voice from heaven. What cause should I take up on your behalf?"

"Don't ask me; ask Da Il." She looked over at Daniel.

Waii burst into raucous laughter. "Him? Come on. Don't tell me you're falling for this charade."

Daniel stood, a measly specimen compared to the buff Waii.

"No meat on your bones, no royal garments. And that scraggly mess you call hair. Seriously?" Waii stopped to look around. "Most importantly, Da Il would be almost as old as me!" Waii raised his voice and pointed at his chest for further emphasis.

"I am Da Il. I am the heir," Daniel replied, but his rebuttal was tentative.

"Okay, prove it." Waii offered the challenge, and, like a sucker, Daniel fell for it. He began to strain his face in an attempt to show some sort of transformative feline features.

"Daniel, don't." Xi attempted to save Daniel from further embarrassment, but it was too late.

Daniel's effort was rewarded with more scorn-filled laughter from Waii. Though his companions considered him a friend and somewhat in the ranks of their leadership, they couldn't help enjoying a laugh at Daniel's expense.

"It seems like not that long ago, you weren't much more than paw-sized yourself," said Xi, hoping to curb Waii's bragging.

"And yet imagine what I could have become if you paid more attention to me," Waii said, rebutting the criticism. "You really believe this is the heir to the throne of Sphinx?"

Xi nodded his reply.

"At my age, I'm going to need more than blind faith," Waii stated.

He picked up a spare leather tunic and tossed it over to Daniel. "You might need to take it in a bit. If by some chance you do manage to show a beast form, we wouldn't want the family jewels to be vulnerable, would we?"

"Have you seen him?" Xi's transition was abrupt, but Waii knew to whom Xi was referring. Yet more conversation only fit for old-kingdom insiders.

"Nope. Look at yourself. That's all the proof you need. He is never coming back. Which makes me wonder why Merlin, the father of all magic, would curse the Gargoyle Clan so, particularly in comparison to the rest of us."

Red and Gray were in earshot and took that as their cue to be elsewhere.

"You're right to be too terrified to even utter his name."

"We are on a quest to restore the old kingdom. Or at least take refuge among what remains. Old kingdom, Commoners, refugees, whatever you want to call us. All of us together. Will you join us?" Xi pleaded.

"Out of many, one." Waii smirked. "I have a few old friends, black panthers, that might want to join us along the way. We head out in the morning."

Out of the corner of his eye, he spotted Phoenix, who was keeping a low profile.

"Unholy ones too? Great. I guess this is one way to go." Waii chuckled. "What kind of cosmic prank was I born into?" he murmured, walking away.

Daniel awoke to morning haze. The sky had only a thin veil of dust clouds, which continued to guard its true expanse. He stood at the entrance to the cave, grateful for the tunic that Waii had given him, for it helped cut the bite of the wind. As he stood there, he saw a short spear with blades at both ends, and recognized it as one of the weapons from Xi's stories.

Daniel glanced around—no one else was awake yet—and picked up the weapon. Both the handle and the blades bore many engravings. He began practicing his drills using the spear. His technique had greatly improved, and he was starting to feel more comfortable with a weapon in his hands.

Five creatures appeared on a nearby ridge—panther-like beasts, black and mysterious as the walking night. They confidently leaped from point to point until they stood in front of Daniel, encircling him. One took a spear from a back holster, threw it into the ground in front of Daniel, and then arched his back and roared. Daniel was fearful but stood his ground.

"Titus!" Waii called out from behind.

He took his animal form and approached Titus. They grabbed opposite forearms then the other set and bumped chest to chest, letting out a shared roar.

"Waii, too soon to see your ugly face," Titus mocked.

They had almost forgotten that Daniel was present. Waii greeted the other black panthers. Titus wanted to get the facts straight. "Did I hear your howls right last night—that you found Da Il?"

"Yes. Panthers, meet Da Il, the royal heir." Waii's introduction was dripping with sarcasm.

"What in the underworld?" replied one of the panthers.

"I know," Waii replied, barely holding back his signature laugh.

"Well, it could be worse," responded Titus.

"Please," said Waii.

"No, I'm just sayin'," Titus replied.

Daniel stiffened his spine. He was slowly becoming less sensitive to the constant humiliation—at least enough to want to save his pride by walking away.

Jessica sat on a nearby rock formation and called out to him. "Daniel, I found something intriguing. I need to take more samples of your blood."

"Maybe later." Daniel moped as he entered the cave. But he stopped as soon as he was barely a few steps in, where he caught a whiff of something unfriendly.

"Waii, did you smell that?" Titus said as he tapped him on the shoulder.

Swiftly, a pack of wolf beasts jumped down from a nearby embankment. One snatched Jessica, and they leaped over the ridge from where they came and disappeared. The group heard her let out a faint, muffled scream.

"No!" Daniel ran out from the cave and headed up the steep incline. Teresa was right there. He leaped on her back, and they raced to the top of the incline.

"Bassa!" Waii yelled, and the large leopard responded.

Waii jumped on Bassa and headed up the peak. Lassa was right behind them with Titus as the rider. Because of their strength, the twin leopards reached the top before Daniel and Teresa. All were caught flat-footed, and most of the camp was still in shock. Grass Mon, Phoenix, and Xi headed up as well to join the pursuit.

"Stay with the camp," Xi instructed his brothers.

Bassa and Lassa were in full pursuit with their riders pushing them hard, but the wolves were fast. With a quick brush of wind, Teresa and Daniel burst out in front. What Teresa lacked in size compared to her peers, she easily made up for in raw speed.

There were five in the pack, and in a flash Teresa caught their slowest teammate and ripped the skin from its back. Daniel leaped off Teresa and began sprinting. It was raw instinct—saving Jessica was all that mattered. He hadn't even realized that he was almost as fast on his own two feet as when he was riding.

He drew his spear. But Jessica's captor was still leading the pack.

Jessica was dangling from its jaws like a rag. Her shawl acted as a noose, and she was in danger of being shaken to death before they would reach whatever destination they had in mind.

Jessica tried to regain a measure of composure. She reached into a back pocket and produced the knife that belonged to Phoenix. The moment when she had received it while they camped flashed across her mind. It was not long after helping Phoenix as they sat together in the cave.

"Do I practice because I'm sick, or am I sick because I practice?" Phoenix had questioned rhetorically.

"Cutting yourself makes your condition worse. I need you to see that. You can be as devout as you choose," Jessica had said gently. "But..." She had reached out her palm. "This part has got to stop."

Jessica's mind snapped back to the present, and she gripped the knife's handle tightly. She stabbed her carrier in the underbelly, and he let go, making only a few steps before circling back in an attempt to retrieve his prize.

The hunter scampered toward Jessica, and Daniel emerged from behind her. He leaped in the air and met the beast with a sharp blow, splitting its head in half right down the center. Teresa leaped in, ready to fight alongside him.

Other hunters rushed in and began to circle them. Daniel used the edge of his boot to pull out the blade that was edged in the fallen wolf. He scowled at the circling party. It was long overdue, and he could feel it surge: the form that had only once occurred was now making its return.

"Come on!" he yelled.

The rush of adrenaline was incredible, but he owned it; he embraced it. His body grew in size and mass. He was now a beast, still with some structure of a man. He clung to his sword, which seemed unnecessary, as he bore large, menacing claws. The wolves prepared to attack, and Daniel roared. The tremendous sound shook the ground, and the pack of wolves was seized with fright, their knees buckling.

Daniel attacked, and two more fell. A few other wolves had ventured a heroic rescue, but were encircled by Waii, Titus, Xi, Grass Mon, and Phoenix. Never had Daniel and his crew wielded such an upper hand. It was sure to send a message once Leonardo's group reached the spot: for the first time, the hunted were the strong ones.

Daniel walked up to the black panthers' leader. In his beast form, Daniel was bigger than all of them. He faced down Titus and threw his spear deep into the ground. Daniel arched his back and growled, shaking the ground more than before. No words were needed; it was clear that he was now the alpha of the pack.

Titus motioned to his fellow panthers, and they lined up in front of Daniel. They morphed into their human forms, something that Waii had not witnessed before. Even to his surprise, they were not more physically fit than Daniel in his human form—just mere lanky, thin, light-skinned youngsters—and they kneeled reverently before the heir apparent.

"Okay, I did not expect that. Did you?" Phoenix ridiculed.

Titus walked over to Waii, who was still in his beast form. "See, it has nothing to do with size. It's all about heart." He then turned and began chanting, "Long live the king! Long live the king!"

Everyone else joined in, except Phoenix, who clapped politely, but did not share their enthusiasm.

Daniel was not caught up in his newfound fame. Instead, he focused on staying mentally present to act as human as possible while wearing the body of a monster. But he began to feel nauseous, and then suddenly came a sharp pain just below his ribs. He reached to pull out a large, dark-blue feather. He looked at it and marveled, wondering how he, a feline beast, could sprout a feather.

Daniel gently tossed it aside. He moved the muscles in his face according to what he remembered to be a smile. He stretched out his hand to Jessica, and saw on her face something he had never seen before. For the first time, she was afraid of him.

CHAPTER 24

HURTFUL HONESTY

"Can you not do that right now?" Jessica blurted in frustration.

The caravan moved along, now a bit larger in size. Jessica had been visibly agitated since Daniel took his form in a decisive victory over the wolves. Nonetheless, he was still caught off guard by the outburst.

"Yeah, sure," Daniel replied softly.

He scooped up the pieces of his sketchbook and walked away. He did not understand—he was sketching her just as before. Seeing Daniel in a way that frightened her caused Jessica to lash out unexpectedly.

"Daniel," she called out apologetically.

"No…I should see how things are progressing." He whistled to Teresa and leaped off the over-mobile and onto her back.

They stuck to the original plan, and cut the use of fuel for most of the vehicles. The gargoyles, the black panthers, and Waii's snow leopards carried out the towing duties. Phoenix was not a fan of being chauffeured around, so she chose to drive one of the three mobiles still burning coal.

The mini talkie in her ear had been buzzing almost nonstop since they entered the wilderness. It worried her. The reception on those little buggers shouldn't be so good that far out of the city. She knew who it was and had no intention of answering.

Daniel encouraged Teresa to ride up next to the front of the over-mobile. Na Mu and Grass Mon sat in the front.

"Hey, big man," Na Mu yelled.

"Hey, Na Mu," replied Daniel, somewhat melancholy.

"That must have been some rush. Wish I were there to see it," Na Mu continued exuberantly.

"It was all right," Daniel responded. "How much farther?"

"Waii says the terrain will keep getting rocky from here on out. But with a steady pace, maybe another five days until we begin to spot some landmarks."

Phoenix pulled up in her mobile at the tail end of the conversation.

"We've lost some time. Do you think your brother will take a shot at us?" Daniel asked.

"That's what I would do," she replied.

"We need to figure out how close he might be. Can you hang back and keep an eye on him?" Grass Mon requested.

"Sure," Phoenix replied.

She didn't mind the assignment. There was now way too much fur and tail in this group for her taste, but this was also akin to asking a reformed alcoholic to supervise his drunken friends.

"Stay out of sight," Grass Mon added.

It wasn't long before she spotted Leonardo's team cresting the ridge. They were fast behind, but the barren, mountainous course was taking a toll on the large group. The twenty-foot silver spire he used to boost his talker signal bobbed hypnotically.

Spotting Leonardo's position and possibilities was an easy task, a boring task. As a vampire who stuck with the Family disciplines only when necessary, Phoenix had never been good at performing simple, boring chores.

Tucked away in one of the several rocky crevices, she was perched in an ideal position, and the wind was on her side. After all, using such a powerful scope on a well-crafted rifle was only truly fulfilling if one intended to use the rest of the weapon.

Despite her position, it would still be a challenging shot, even for a trained vampire assassin. She began to wonder if she could hit a target from that distance.

She pulled the trigger.

"Yes!" she shouted, completely giddy. There was laughing, and even a little dance.

The drone vampire fell to the ground as the bullet pierced his temple, and with the use of a silencer, the confused bunch had no idea where the shot came from. The mini talkie rang, and she answered.

"I really liked...what's his name," voiced Leonardo.

They both laughed. For a moment, they were just siblings again.

"Why don't you just turn around and go back to South Central? You're embarrassing yourself," Phoenix teased.

"Are you kidding? I'm having way too much fun," Leonardo replied.

But through her scope, she could see that wasn't entirely the case. His face bore dark heat blotches, and his armor betrayed hot patches of sticky sweat underneath.

Phoenix kept just ahead of Leonardo, always out of sight. Every now and then, she took another shot at Leonardo's forces, taking out an inspector surveying the trail or an idle drone. Increasingly, the hypnotic effect of the antenna dulled her senses. She was so caught up in taking potshots that she forgot to check in with the caravan.

⊫⊪

They made yet another stop at a small cave to provide drinking water for the large felines and weary travelers.

When Jessica reached the small, rocky cave, she let out a big sigh as she set down her heavy backpack. She dropped to her knees, and covered her face with her hands.

"I can't do this anymore," she exhaled, rocking back and forth. Tears rolled down her cheeks. "It's too much. I can't do this."

After a time, her movement stilled, and she gave another, deep sigh. She opened the heavy backpack and began to toss away the numerous research materials she had accumulated. Her load was half-empty already when she got to the canvas pouch that held the liquid-filled glass containers. She pulled out the stopper of one, but then froze when she noticed what was inside.

"Oh my God," Jessica gasped.

When she turned and stood, an older man appeared in front of her, so close that she almost bumped into him. He wore a cloak made of cobalt-blue silk that was embroidered with golden stars and a matching, cone-shaped hat. It was unlike anything she had ever seen. His hair was white and flowed like mist, and his skin glowed amber. Even the air around him shimmered.

"Hello, my dear," he said gently, yet he carried a gravitas that made Jessica's heart tremble.

Jessica stepped back. "Who are you?" Her voice shook.

"An old friend," he replied.

He reached for his cap and took it off. His long, wispy hair receded from the crest of his head. The old man turned his back to Jessica and took a few steps toward a jagged stone that jutted from the cave wall. He took a seat and a weary breath.

"Don't worry; I didn't expect you to recognize me. I haven't had to intervene much on your behalf. Your parents did a mighty fine job raising you despite the limited time they had.

"When I first saw you, I thought you were perfect. Magic doesn't scare you at all—it's simply science working with subtlety, right? With that scientific mind applied to a love of animals, I couldn't have planned it better myself.

"I know you were mad at Daniel, but you would never leave him. Especially after what you've just discovered. Honestly, I don't know what he would do without you. Do not tempt me into taking that risk."

Jessica desperately wanted to run, but her legs felt like wet noodles beneath her.

"I probably don't need to explain who I am; at this very second, I have chosen to reveal myself for one purpose." He raised his head and looked at her intently, noting the intense concentration on her face as she worked out the mystery of who he was.

The old man looked at the small glass beaker that Jessica held in her hand. She followed his gaze, and watched in horror as the liquid boiled without becoming hot, and then threatened to overflow the container. Jessica let go of the beaker, and it shattered on the stone floor; the spill converted the area to glass.

"The link between science and magic is a wonderful thing," he commented.

"I have to tell Daniel," Jessica stated.

"No. You cannot." The old man stood and walked toward Jessica, although his feet did not actually touch the ground. "It's too soon, and he is just not ready."

"He needs to know the truth."

"Yes, he does, but he also has to meet his destiny. Unless the time is right and all the pieces are in place, Daniel will simply not be willing to do what is required. And this is not just about him."

"Daniel!" Jessica screamed, and she dodged, trying to get around the old man.

He grabbed her by the elbow, and Jessica was immediately transformed into a statue of crystal.

"I'm sorry, my dear," he said softly and vanished.

"Dad was the best, wasn't he?" Leonardo said.

The siblings were still wrapped in their conversation.

"How would you know? Did you ever have any alone time with the guy?" Phoenix asked derisively.

"Yeah, you're right; he was a prick," Leonardo replied. "But he sent the best stuff. Always seemed to know exactly what we needed and when. You know, he was there. Through the gifts and stuff. That's more than Daniel had."

"Don't tell me you're obsessed with Daniel too?"

"It's all about Daniel now. Dad told me to focus on that skinny little runt," said Leonardo. "That's right. I heard from dear old Dad. He called just to speak to me."

"What are you talking about?" Phoenix looked through the scope to check his facial expression, trying to detect a bluff.

"It seems we have more in common with Daniel than we first thought. Didn't he tell you?" Her silence told Leonardo all he needed to know. "Either Daniel didn't tell you, or he doesn't know. This is precious. Poor kid."

Phoenix listened intently for hours, not even resting her eyes from the scope once. Unbeknown to her, the antennae had been modified to emit a trance-inducing signal through Leonardo's talkie.

"Phoenix, what are you doing?" It was Grass Mon.

She got up hurriedly, dusting off her clothes, in a daze.

"Phoenix, why didn't you check in? Never mind. We have to go." Grass Mon glanced down the ridge. "Oh, no. He's too close."

"Grass Mon, I have to tell you something," Phoenix said nervously, barely emerging from her dreamlike state.

"Not now! Get in."

They both got in the mobile that Grass Mon had arrived in, and they abandoned hers. Grass Mon floored the pedal, and big plumes of smoke bellowed from the exhausts.

The sky was filled with patchy dust clouds, which made the perfect cover for a squadron of bat vampires to gain a tactical advantage. As Phoenix and Grass Mon roared into the desert, the squadron gave up their cover to make their move.

"And that's not all," the talkie hissed in Phoenix's ear. "Dad said if I capture and kill Daniel, he will give me half the estate and controlling interest in this entire region."

"We have incoming!" Grass Mon pointed to the bats, upon which assassin vampires were riding.

Phoenix drew her rifle and opened fire. She hit one but only after firing many rounds. Unlike last time, they were on their guard against her.

Three assassins dropped from the sky and landed on the mobile. Grass Mon kept one hand on the wheel and engaged the assassin on the hood in a sword duel. Phoenix faced off in a two-against-one match with the other assassins. She stood on the back of the mobile as the match heated up. The bumpy driving and uneven course threatened a wipeout.

The vehicle became airborne for a second after hitting a miniature ridge, but no one missed a beat. The combat was poetic and swift on both fronts. It was beautiful to watch except for the fact that both of their lives depended on ending it quickly.

Phoenix landed a midair spin-kick that sent one opponent flying. She landed on the edge of the mobile just before missing the vehicle. However, there was no time to feel the thrill that came from connecting on that since she still needed to contend with the other. And the other airborne assassins were gaining on them.

"You do know you won't make it out of this one alive, right, sis?" Leonardo was still a bug in her ear. "With this rocky terrain, it might still be a day before the rest of my forces can catch up to Daniel. But I have given these assassins the task of making sure that you don't breathe another day. Traitor!"

The ringleader of the remaining bat vampires gave a loud shriek, and two more riders dove for the already tasked mobile. Then the lead assassin took his bat into a kamikaze dive, striking the front of the vehicle so that the metal shattered, and the mobile took a swan leap into the air. All the variables were too much for Grass Mon to track, and his opponent took the small opening to pierce him in the side.

"Kudos," Grass Mon congratulated him, and then dismembered the assassin.

Apparently, a midair, out-of-control scenario was no big obstacle for either party. Even the severely injured

Grass Mon stuck a somersault landing as the mobile crashed, totaled a few feet away.

Phoenix stood back to back with him, using her rifle as a bar shield and club in close range. She swung the rifle by its strap to add additional range.

They were winning, somehow. Phoenix was about to put the finishing touches on her third victim when she heard Grass Mon let out a gasp. He had fallen, hunching to his knees, and his opponent ran a blade right through his back until the tip bit into the sand below.

Phoenix spun the assassin around, grabbing him by the throat. She pulled the blade from Grass Mon's back and rammed it through the assassin's gut. She then spat in its face, and the skin began to sizzle and burn. She withdrew the sword and hurled it at the remaining assassin, imbedding it deep in his throat.

"Baby, baby, just hold on," she whispered as she kneeled beside her beloved.

Grass Mon began to gasp, and green fluid drained from his mouth. He made a gurgling sound as he tried to speak, but the words could not come out.

She spotted Bassa and Lassa approaching, ridden by Na Mu and Waii.

"Hold on. Do it for me, okay?" She began to rock him in her arms.

He coughed up some more fluid. "It's better this way. When you're cured, I might have wanted to eat you. Then where would we be?" His eyes began to glaze over.

"No! Grass Mon!" she yelled.

Bassa arrived. Na Mu dismounted and began to administer CPR. But Grass Mon's eyes were closed, and no breath rose from him. Na Mu ripped a piece of his shirt, and attempted to clot the wound.

"Apply some pressure, here," Na Mu instructed Phoenix as he continued joint-fist CPR on Grass Mon's chest.

"You didn't come all the way out here to die on us, did you?" Na Mu said, but he didn't respond. "Let's try to get him back to the others."

They hoisted him onto Bassa's back and rode quickly. The sun finally broke through the clouds, just as it began to set.

They reached the group's small, open camp by nightfall, and rushed Grass Mon into a tent, but kept Phoenix on the outside. Perhaps it was for the best, but she could still see their silhouettes through the fabric of the tent by the light of lamps inside, and that seemed more than she could bear. She knew the results even before Waii made his way out to deliver the news.

"No!" She let out a loud, piercing scream.

Daniel made the mistake of approaching from behind to place a consoling hand on her shoulder. She turned and pushed him with both hands, then did so again.

Phoenix made for the tent. Na Mu came out and intercepted her, throwing his arms around her, and the vampire tears began to flow.

Most thought that vampires were incapable of emotion. But it wasn't the case. They buried all feelings deep within their psyches. Few things could tap such a deep well of emotion. Her screams were like that of a banshee. Phoenix's bloodshot eyes flowed teardrops of literal acid that singed both her clothes and Na Mu's arms.

⊨⊢ ⊣⊨

Later that night, they made camp. It was a brief opportunity to rest, as the next day they were sure to be hard-pressed to stay ahead.

Daniel sat in a tent, staring at Jessica's crystallized form by the dim, ambient light. His eyes burned as tears streamed down.

The slightly unveiled sky rumbled, and storm clouds gathered. Na Mu stood several feet away from Daniel's tent. He wrapped Grass Mon's body ceremoniously in a dark tarp and began strapping it to the back of the over-mobile. Na Mu picked up his master's twin swords, first thinking to place them with the body, prepped for burial. He paused as a memory flooded his mind.

"If I die, I want you to promise me," Grass Mon had said. He stood, holding a firm grip on the hand of his number-one general. "Promise that you will not bury these swords with me, for they are alive, and will live forever."

In the memory, Na Mu watched from the sidelines with a few others while Grass Mon anointed Number One, his chosen successor. He knelt and picked up the swords lying on the ground.

"I swear," Number One had replied.

At that moment, Na Mu held the swords reverently. He found the x-shaped holster for the swords and placed them in each sleeve. Na Mu strapped the holder over his shoulders and rose to his feet. In one motion, he drew both swords and wielded them swiftly, making a sudden stop—a quick, flawless drill of drawing double swords to engage in battle. He had seen Grass Mon practice the drill many times, and he rehearsed it in secret almost as many.

"I swear," Na Mu vowed.

At the other end of camp, the carved-stone gargoyle brothers knelt facing each other. They held their wings outstretched, almost touching, as they clasped their hands and closed their eyes. The three chanted and groaned in an effort to connect with the supernatural.

"Hear our prayer," said Xi as he raised his head. "Why do you hate us and work against us? Give us hearts of flesh. Lift the curse and restore our clans."

His brothers continued to chant, synchronizing with his spoken prayers. The dark clouds began to drift down toward the earth, and there was a sound of thunder.

Daniel walked over to Jessica, and he gently touched the form of her face. It was cold, and the faceted surface acted as a prism. He could see through her.

Phoenix stealthily entered and grabbed Daniel by his collar, hauling him to an open area. She then placed a pistol to his temple. The camp started to stir as some realized what was happening. The gargoyles were caught off guard, not expecting an attack from within.

They rushed into action but did not attack. "I knew you couldn't be trusted," hissed Red.

"Funny coming from you," Phoenix replied.

"Phoenix, please, don't do this," said Na Mu, pleading for Daniel's life. "It won't bring Grass Mon back."

"Go ahead, do it. Put me out of my misery," responded Daniel.

He knelt on the ground. Phoenix stood behind him with the muzzle of her pistol wading through Daniel's scruffy blond hair. Although she was acting out of grief, his resignation was unexpected, and she knew he wasn't bluffing.

"You're right. This isn't to bring him back—this is for me. I'm finished with all of you. I'm going to kill you, Daniel, and return to my family. For real this time."

She cocked the pistol, but hesitated. Tears flooded furiously to the surface of her eyes. "But before you die, you deserve to know the truth."

Phoenix looked over at Xi. "Fakes! Hypocrites! Every single one of you. Tell him the truth—tell him everything."

Daniel supposed this was just as good an ending as any. A life of struggle, pain, and loneliness cut short by ones who believed him to be greater than what he believed. But there were forces at work, doing what could not be seen, fulfilling things he could not perform. If only Daniel had the will to go on just a little farther.

www.ingramcontent.com/pod-product-compliance
Lightning Source LLC
Chambersburg PA
CBHW051244260626
47162CB00002B/605